About the Author

Omotayo D. Alabi has over twenty years of experience working in the humanitarian sector. He has worked in management and advisory capacity on food security, agriculture and rural development, farm management, green and resilience economy, and income, market, and digital economy. He has also actively worked addressing environmental, conservation, and sustainability issues in refugee and returnee camps in many countries including Sierra Leone, Liberia, Sudan, Nigeria, and South Sudan. He has experience either working or consulting for the European Union, UNFAO, UNDP, UNCDF, Concern Worldwide, Catholic Relief Services, Plan International, Welthungerhilfe, Environmental Foundation for Africa and a host of other NGOs.

He is the MD of Agcrest Development Centre. Mr Alabi worked with Agrer Belgium as a Technical Adviser on Agronomist Extension for the Technical Assistance for Increased Agriculture Production of Smallholders in South Sudan at the EU Delegation South Sudan. He did undergraduate studies in Agriculture Extension and Management at the Ahmadu Bello University, Nigeria, holds a Graduate Certificate in Sustainable Development from the University of Exeter, United Kingdom; a Certificate in Business Sustainability Management from the University of Cambridge, United Kingdom; and a Master of Science in Programme and Project Management from the University of Chester, United Kingdom.

Dedication

To all individuals (living or dead) who support vulnerable and marginalised people around the world.

Omotayo D. Alabi

BRINGING THE PHILANTHROPY PROJECT IN YOU TO LIFE

How to Start a Charity and Make it Work, Your First Few Steps to Impacting Lives and Managing your Project

AUSTIN MACAULEY PUBLISHERS
LONDON * CAMBRIDGE * NEW YORK * SHARJAH

Copyright © Omotayo D. Alabi 2025

The right of Omotayo D. Alabi to be identified as author of this work has been asserted by the author in accordance with sections 77 and 78 of the Copyright, Designs and Patents Act 1988.

All rights reserved. No part of this publication may be reproduced, stored in a retrieval system, or transmitted in any form or by any means, electronic, mechanical, photocopying, recording, or otherwise, without the prior permission of the publishers.

Any person who commits any unauthorised act in relation to this publication may be liable to criminal prosecution and civil claims for damages.

This is a work of fiction. Names, characters, businesses, places, events, locales and incidents are either the products of the author's imagination or used in a fictitious manner. Any resemblance to actual persons, living or dead, or actual events is purely coincidental.

A CIP catalogue record for this title is available from the British Library.

ISBN 9781035868971 (Paperback)
ISBN 9781035868988 (ePub e-book)

www.austinmacauley.com

First Published 2025
Austin Macauley Publishers Ltd®
1 Canada Square
Canary Wharf
London
E14 5AA

Acknowledgements

I would like to thank everyone who took out time to talk to me and share their experiences in workshops, brainstorming sessions, and training sessions, as well as the vast numbers of project participants who have allowed me access to their communities and their spaces over the course of my work as a humanitarian worker.

I owe a lot of the information presented here to many of my colleagues, who through various interactions have shed light on a number of areas essential to NGO operations. My appreciation to Alistair Short, Brid Barret, Manoj Kumar, Patrick Wamala, Wale Osofisan, Tommy Garnet, Paolo Girlando, Richard Lambol, Paula Connolly, John Sugden, Steve Hind, Mou Ambrose Thiik, Paul Wagstaff, Tonderayi Makumire, Charles Hopkins, and many too numerous to mention here for the tutelage, encouragement, and support received from working together.

Let me also acknowledge especially the contribution from Kendra Brassfield and Mary A. M for their substantial and direct input given for this book. They could be my co-authors on this project. I thank both of them for the reviews, pieces contributed, and for collating and sharing very vital lessons from their experiences in the field and from other sources, many of which they have graciously allowed me to incorporate into this book. I sincerely thank friends and colleagues who also read the manuscript, critiqued, edited, and proofread it to shape it into what it is.

It is indeed still a work in progress.

My gratitude also goes to the institutions/organisations/companies (e.g., NGOs, academia, UN agencies, embassies, governments, and donors) who have given me employment (full or part-time) at one time or another. Through the platform they provided me, I've had wonderful learning and enriching experiences in my over twenty years of working in the humanitarian sector. Many of them I reference in this book.

My appreciation also goes to my lovely family (Omowumi, Tunde, Kayode, Adeola and Lekan) and siblings for their support and understanding throughout my career. I cannot appreciate enough the sacrifices you have made, and how you have coped and managed in my absence, and during my stay in the field. Above all, to God for making this possible.

Omotayo Daud'Alabi

Table of Contents

Introduction	11
Chapter 1: Finding Your Passion	14
Gaining Clarity by Asking Yourself the Hard Questions	20
Chapter 2: Getting Started	30
Chapter 3: Legally Establishing Your Charity	43
The Frameworks	43
What are the Benefits of Legally Establishing Your Charity?	53
Chapter 4: Creating a Strategic Plan	59
The Components of a Strategic Plan	61
Chapter 5: Systems and Processes	75
Policies and Procedures	77
Financial Systems	77
Human Resources Policies	78
Developing Standard Operating Procedures	80
Chapter 6: Budgeting and Financials	88
Distinguish Nonprofit Budgeting from For-Profit Budgeting	96
Break Down Your Budget Components	97
Fixed Budget Reviews	98
Forecasting Future Income and Expenses	107

Chapter 7: Fundraising   110

Chapter 8: Marketing and Communications   120

   Developing a Brand   *120*

Chapter 9: Team Building   126

Chapter 10: Volunteer Force   135

Chapter 11: Evaluating Your Progress   141

Chapter 12: Weathering the Storm   150

Chapter 13: Measuring Impact and Success   165

Chapter 14: Sustaining Your Success   176

Bibliography   186

Introduction

There's a little generosity (call it philanthropy if you may) in every one of us. The desire to help and support each other is fundamental to the survival of our families, communities, nations, and indeed the human race. Empathy, reaching out, and giving back—though often a choice—have always existed and will continue to do so. As the global population increases and our inability to sustain global natural resources persists, along with widening poverty gaps and the attendant consequences of climate change, we will all be vulnerable at one time or another. With this reality, it is becoming more apparent that helping each other will become the norm.

The difference is (and will be) the way we're set up to provide for people in need of assistance and/or helping hands. As we move away from the informal ways of supporting each other as members of the same family and communities into small charities or non-governmental organisations (NGO), what once started as voluntary endeavours, responding to needs mainly in the global South, has become a crucial global sector.

Although there's no agreement on which was the first organised international NGO, reference is however often made to the Anti-Slavery Society, which was formed in 1839 followed by International Committee of the Red Cross (ICRC) in 1863. This was before the United Nations was established in 1945. ICRC started work in Israel and the occupied territories in 1948. Regarding the ways NGOs are affecting our everyday lives, we often hear about the Red Cross and its activities, which involve saving lives on war fronts and disaster areas; we also hear about how the World Food Programme of the United Nations along with partners, responding to emergencies and helping people experiencing food insecurity around the globe.

There are perhaps millions of charities/NGOs around the world doing good and responding to people in need. We found 54,726 NGOs registered on the Worldwide NGO Directory published online by the World Association of Non-

Governmental Organisations (WANGO). Their distribution is presented in the table below.

Table 1: Number of Charities/NGOs around the world

Regions	Registered NGOs
South America	665
Oceania	658
West Africa	2,375
Central America	338
Eastern Africa	1,289
Northern Africa	231
Central Africa	562
Southern Africa	448
Northern America	23,137
Caribbean	486
Eastern Asia	408
Southeastern Asia	987
Southern Europe	1,099
South Central Asia	4,396
Western Asia	795
Eastern Europe	8,362
Northern Europe	4,694
Western Europe	3,796

Source: WANGO 2022

Some examples of NGOs include Concern Worldwide, World Vision, Mercy Corps, Plan International, Care International, Norwegian Refugee Council, Welthungerhilfe, OXFAM, and International Rescue Committee, to mention a few. The difference an NGO is able to make in delivering aid and assistance to those in dire need depends on the way they're structured and the resources available to them.

You would think there are sufficient charities in the world, but going by the numbers in the table above, unfortunately, that isn't true; there are still so many people in need of help and assistance who are yet to be reached. Some of them are staring us in our faces, hidden in plain sight. Many people are traumatised, hungry, overweight, and unemployed, many face gender-based violence daily and others have mental health issues and need our support. We all have a significant role to play and a duty of care. Our contributions to humanity are among what makes the world go round, one that stands out and is highly appreciated.

Many people have reached out to me, asking how they can set up an NGO, a community-based organisation, or a private charity. In this book, based on my twenty-years-plus experience working in the humanitarian sector, I've itemised and discussed some of what I consider the most important aspects of charity/NGO setup. I've also included basic project operation management tips you should consider to make your charity more impactful. Charity and NGO are interchangeably used throughout this book. The opinions expressed in this book are solely mine and do not necessarily represent the views of any organisation or individual cited.

My hope is you will find this book useful as you set up and run your own charity, extending a helping hand to others. We are in this together!

Chapter 1
Finding Your Passion

Passion is the engine that drives us to excellence. It propels everything, including our vision, mission, and aspirations. It makes us want to get up each morning and do something that matters.

It's the one thing that drives us to make a difference in the world. Without passion, we would go through the day without real purpose.

Many of the charities you hear about today were founded by individuals, partners, or organisations that were passionate about helping people in need and to contribute their own quota to helping humanity. Mother Teresa is top of the pack and a household name whenever we discuss charities and talk about people who have followed their passion and calling to support humanity.

Another such person is Henry Dunant, who brought into being the Red Cross movement you know of today. He started out with a passion for helping wounded soldiers in the Battle of Solferino in 1859 and then lobbied political leaders to take more action to protect war victims. It is said that 'the Battle of Solferino (24 June 1859) was the decisive episode in the struggle for Italian unification'. Dunant's two main ideas were for a treaty that would oblige armies to care for all wounded soldiers and for the creation of national societies that would help provide military medical services. What a noble thought!

As the son of late military personnel, I can identify with this objective. There were times we waited for our daddy to return home safely. No family of a soldier wants to be informed they'll never see their father or loved ones again.

Concern Worldwide, an Irish-based charity that started as African Concern, was birthed by Kay O'Loughlin Kennedy and John O'Loughlin Kennedy in 1968. They did this in response to the famine they saw ravaging vulnerable people in Biafra, Nigeria. Both Kennedys have their roots in Catholic mission. Their desire to support the families of the then-starving Biafran soldiers in Southeastern Nigeria, fighting for succession, before any outsider could move in to help or offer unbiased assistance, remains highly relevant and appreciated. The Irish people so generously supported the vision of these two founders that Concern Worldwide has since expanded to other continents, providing lifesaving support to the poor and most vulnerable.

OXFAM was founded in the United Kingdom by a group of international NGOs, the name 'OXFAM' comes from the Oxford Committee for Famine Relief, founded in Britain in 1942. The group campaigned for food supplies to be sent through an allied naval blockade to starving women and children in enemy-occupied Greece during the Second World War. OXFAM International is now a global movement and a prominent charity, doing what it does best: fighting inequality and injustice and relieving hunger and poverty around the world.

You may have heard about these big NGOs, but maybe a little less about others who are by no means less important despite not being on the front pages of newspapers, news headlines, or among the first in your search engine algorithms. One such is the Hellen Keller Foundation. The story of Helen Keller is that of courage and hope; she became the first blind-deaf person to effectively communicate with the sighted and hearing world. Helen Keller International was cofounded in 1915 by two extraordinary individuals, Helen Keller and George Kessler, to assist soldiers blinded during their service in the First World War.

Another is Marie Stopes International (MSI), founded by three reproductive health practitioners—Tim Black, Jean Black, and Phil Harvey—in 1976, with a mission to bring choice to women around the world. MSI makes the bold claim, "We are unapologetically pro-choice: we believe every woman and every girl should have the power to decide and determine the path their life takes."

Smaller yet similar charities have sprung up over the years, rising to the occasion, making a huge difference, and contributing immeasurably to humanity—as we saw during the COVID-19 pandemic of 2020. Some of the charities are formally registered but many are not and have still served countless homeless people with hot meals and handed out blankets and sheets. Some people have even readily given up a few empty rooms in their houses to help others with shelter, sank water wells, taught children how to read and write, paid fees, or bought school uniforms for children on the streets of the Americas, Africa, Europe, and Asia.

Other NGOs with similar missions have provided first-aid, and their volunteers have gone out to help dig out those trapped in the rubble from earthquakes, tsunamis, or landslides in Nepal, Haiti, Indonesia, and the Philippines. The names of founders who have shown such incredible levels of passion and heart for doing good are too numerous to mention here, but what makes them stand out is 'Passion', a common denominator.

'Finding your passion' is a journey that can take time and it's rarely as simple as 'just do what you love'. It requires an honest assessment of who we are, the skills we possess, and our resources. Every human being has a unique and special purpose only they can fulfil. Our passion makes us come alive, but it's also about being in the right place at the right time to make a difference.

I believe you have what it takes to be in this category—visionary, kind individuals willing to help—and/or that you're trying to figure out how you can channel your passion into helping humanity. My little contribution is to (together) walk you through the nitty-gritty of how you will not only set up your first charity/NGO but run it successfully.

Part of being passionate is understanding the reality of what can be done. It's not just enthusiasm and goodwill that's needed but also a realistic plan to get things done. Think about it, every day. As we walk down the street and through our lives, we come across opportunities to make a difference. There are always one or more things that really nag us and for which we think we could do something. These are the sparks of passion, and if you pay attention to them, they can lead you down a path of doing something meaningful with your life.

Sometimes we think we need big skills or a lot of money to make a difference, but that's not necessarily true. What it takes is dedication and commitment to doing what's necessary. Be realistic, knowing you alone cannot solve the entire world's problems, but you can contribute to fixing a tiny bit of it. If everyone plays their part and does their bit, we could easily fix the many seemingly insurmountable problems facing mankind, knowing we're all in this together.

NGOs are independent organisations that work to address social, economic, and environmental issues around the world. These organisations often operate in areas where governments are (in most cases) unable or unwilling to provide resources for diverse reasons and they often work closely with local communities to develop solutions to pressing issues. Over the years, NGOs have played a critical role in responding to a wide range of crises and calamities around the world, from natural disasters to armed conflicts, to health epidemics, to economic downturns, to contemporary social issues such as the denial of citizens their citizenship, as we have seen recently with the Rohingya people of Myanmar. At the core of all these cases are people with passion and people willing to help through their resources, ability, or sheer will.

One example of how NGOs have intervened in a critical situation is the response to the 2010 earthquake in Haiti. After the earthquake struck, hundreds of NGOs rushed to provide humanitarian aid, including food, water, shelter, and medical care. Many of the organisations work closely with local communities to assess their needs and develop the long-term solutions needed to provide relief to the people in need and find the right mechanisms to rebuild the country. In the course of their interventions, NGOs such as Partners in Health, Concern Worldwide, and many others, for instance, have worked closely with the Haitian Government and local communities to rebuild healthcare facilities, train healthcare workers, and improve access to healthcare in rural areas.

Another example of how NGOs have responded to critical situations is the Ebola outbreak in West Africa in 2014. The outbreak, which spread to Guinea, Sierra Leone, and Liberia, led to over eleven thousand deaths and had a devastating impact on the region. In response, a number of NGOs worked to provide healthcare and other essential services to those affected by the disease. For example, the NGO Médecins Sans Frontières/Doctors Without Borders (MSF) deployed teams of healthcare workers to the region to provide medical care, and the organisations Save the Children, OXFAM, and World Vision worked to provide essential supplies, such as food and water, to those in need.

Concern Worldwide was at the forefront, helping households cope with their misery that came with Ebola through the provision of health advisory services, psychosocial services, and giving people decent burials—a task definitely not for the faint-hearted. Plan International, Catholic Relief Service, Christian Aid, Handicap International, Islamic Relief, and World Vision have remained at the forefront in supporting children and their families to cope by supplying relief items (food and non-food items) throughout the crises. Volunteer Services Organisation also deployed volunteer experts to provide institutions with critical, relevant, and professional manpower.

NGOs have also played a critical role in responding to economic crises around the world. For example, when the global financial crisis struck in 2008, many NGOs worked to provide financial assistance and other support to those most affected by the crisis. For example, the NGO Microfinanzas Internacional worked to provide microloans to small businesses in developing countries, helping stimulate economic growth and reduce poverty. Similarly, OXFAM worked to provide financial education and other support to affected individuals and communities, helping build resilience and improve financial stability.

NGOs have also played a crucial role in responding to natural disasters around the world. For example, after the 2011 earthquake and tsunami in Japan, a number of NGOs rushed to provide assistance to those affected by the disaster. These organisations provided a range of services, including food, water, shelter, and medical care, and they worked closely with local communities to assess their needs and develop long-term solutions to rebuild the affected areas. In addition, NGOs such as the Red Cross and Save the Children in many situations have played a critical role in responding to other natural disasters around the world, including hurricanes, floods, and earthquakes.

NGOs have also played a key role in responding to conflicts and other violent situations. For example, after the Syrian conflict began in 2011 and the conflict in Gaza Strip which began in 2024, a number of NGOs rushed to provide humanitarian aid to those affected by the conflict. These organisations provided a range of services, including food, water, shelter, and medical care, and they worked closely with local communities to assess their needs and develop long-term solutions to rebuild the affected areas. In addition, NGOs such as Amnesty International and Human Rights Watch have played a critical role in documenting and addressing human rights violations in conflict-affected areas around the world.

In South Sudan, the struggle for independence endured for over forty years before it was finally achieved in 2011. The effects of the war resulted in the destruction of basic infrastructure, which exacerbated issues of hunger to the level of famine in some locations and to the extent that during the April-July 2023 lean season "about two-thirds of the South Sudanese population (7.76 million people) are likely to face acute food insecurity while 1.4 million children will be malnourished." This is a sad set of statistics and a compelling situation for the people of South Sudan. Information such as this comes in handy when you're choosing what to do and how to help.

Responding to the crisis in South Sudan, UN Agencies such as the Food and Agriculture Organisation (FAO), the United Nations International Children Emergency Fund (UNICEF) now known as the United Nations Children's Fund, and the World Food Programme (WFP) and NGOs, e.g., Norwegian Peoples Aid, World Concern; Norwegian Refugee Council, Veterinarian Sans Frontier (VSF) Germany, VSF Suisse, VSF Canada, VSF Belgium; Concern Worldwide, Plan International, War Child, World Concern, Mercy Corp, Care International, Internal Rescue Committee, Islamic Relief, and so many more international and national NGOs too numerous to mention here with the support of the UN agencies (WFP, UNHCR, IOM, FAO, UNOCHA, UNIDO, OCHA, UNESCO, and UNICEF) were called to action to intervene and help.

The donor community such as the European Union, USAID, the Kingdom of Netherlands, Canadian Foreign Aid, Japanese Aid, Norwegian Agency for Development Cooperation (NORAD), BMZ-Germany, African Development Bank, and UK Aid often provide the bulk of the emergency and development assistance needed. Individual foundations like the Bill and Melinda Gates Foundation also provided funds. In a crisis such as this one, a roll call of non-governmental organisations (NGOs), United Nations agencies (UN), and donors who have intervened could be indicative of the severity of the problem, available funding streams and the interest of donors. Many NGOs are actively involved in advocacy and working with both governments and communities to find solutions to core problems such as water and sanitation, environmental restoration, climate change, human and women's rights, demining, and disability. Water Aid, ICRC, Environmental Foundation for Africa (EFA), UNICEF, Mining Action Group, Greenpeace, Birdlife International, International Union for Conservation of Nature (IUCN), Conservation International, Flora and Fauna International, and many more are all actively working towards achieving the Sustainable Development Goals and actively participating in the various conferences of the parties prominent in this space.

There are also wonderful individuals as champions, such as Jane Goodall, Wangari Maathai, Chico Mendes, David Brower, George Washington Carver, and many more, working in this field.

In conclusion, NGOs have played a vital role in responding to a wide range of critical situations and calamities around the world. These organisations have provided essential aid and support to people affected by natural disasters, conflicts, and economic crises, as well as those facing other pressing issues, and they have worked closely with local communities to develop short- and long-term solutions to problems affecting people and their communities. Government and NGO interventions have helped but human needs, desires, and goals are many.

As you would have noted from the UN Development Goals, there are still a lot of needs to meet and work to do—for which your contribution will be much needed and appreciated. This leads us to the question of how does one identify their passion? To help guide you through answering this all-important question, I found the five-part checklist very helpful.

The Five-Part Checklist

As much as we all want to do something good in the world, it's important we check within ourselves to make sure we're in a position to make a difference. It doesn't necessarily mean you have to give up everything else and go all in, but it does mean taking the time to ensure you can do something good without sacrificing too much. If one starts sacrificing their personal life, the future of good work or charity will be limited.

Here's a five-part checklist for assessing if you're ready to pursue your passion.

Gaining Clarity by Asking Yourself the Hard Questions

Gaining clarity can be a difficult and overwhelming process but it's essential for both personal and professional growth. One way to gain clarity is by asking yourself the hard questions. These are the questions that may be uncomfortable or difficult to confront but they can help you understand yourself and your goals more deeply. Here are some examples of hard questions you can ask yourself to gain clarity:

What do I really want in life? This question can be difficult to answer because it requires you to think about your values, goals, and aspirations. It's easy to get caught up in the day-to-day demands of life and lose sight of what you truly want. Take some time to reflect on what truly matters to you and what you want to achieve.

What am I willing to sacrifice to achieve my goals? Achieving your goals often requires sacrifice. You may need to give up certain activities or relationships to focus on your goals. Ask yourself what you're willing to sacrifice to achieve your goals.

What are my priorities? It's easy to get caught up in the busyness of life and lose sight of what's truly important. Take some time to think about what's most important to you and make sure your actions and choices reflect your priorities.

How do I define success? Success means different things to different people. What does success mean to you? Is it about achieving certain goals or is it about feeling fulfilled and satisfied with your life?

What are my strengths and weaknesses? Understanding your strengths and weaknesses can help you make informed decisions about your career and personal life. Take some time to think about what you're naturally good at and where you may need to work a little harder. What are my values? Your values are the things most important to you. They guide your decisions and shape your actions. Take some time to think about what your values are and how they influence your choices.

What do I really want out of this situation? Sometimes it can be helpful to take a step back and consider what you really want out of a situation. Are you looking for a specific outcome or are you more focused on the process?

As mentioned above, asking yourself these hard questions can be difficult but it's an essential part of the process of gaining clarity. It can be helpful to write down your answers or discuss them with someone you trust. By taking the time to reflect on these questions, you can gain a better understanding of yourself and your goals, which can help you to make more informed and confident decisions.

It all begins with some soul-searching. Asking yourself the hard questions can help you gain clarity and better understand what truly motivates you. The following are some examples of these questions:

- What would I do with my life if money was no object?
- What brings me joy?
- What values should guide my decision-making?
- How will this contribute to the greater good?

In essence, these might seem simple questions but if we go into the details and answer them honestly, it can help us gain clarity into our passions and what we truly care about.

For instance, if your passion is alleviating poverty and you do some soul-searching, you might realise it's about giving people the tools to build better lives for themselves. And with this knowledge in hand, you can start exploring ways to make a difference through more meaningful and effective means.

Time Commitment

Once we have clarity on our passions, it's time to assess if we have enough time each week to devote to making a difference. It's too easy to get overwhelmed by our daily obligations and other responsibilities, leaving little time to make a difference.

There are only twenty-four hours a day, and it's important to ensure you're leaving enough time for yourself, your family, and your friends. But if you can manage to set aside some time each week (even a few hours), it can help you get closer to making a difference. Someone who works sixty hours a week and takes care of their family might not be able to make a difference in the way someone with more time can.

With regard to intervening in humanitarian situations, timing is crucial. Often practitioners, donors, and philanthropists are unprepared or ill-prepared to respond during emergencies when a calamity is announced. People in vulnerable situations require more urgent need and immediate attention than you probably think. They require food, medicine, water, and shelter. In mobilising resources, supply chain issues often become stretched and could delay what's meant to be delivered.

What Can You Bring to the Cause?

It's not just about having the time and resources to make a difference—it's also about understanding what skills and talents we can offer. Do you have any special skills or experience you can bring to the cause? For instance, if your passion is helping those in need, perhaps you have great organisational skills. Or maybe you're an excellent public speaker who can help with fundraising efforts.

As a potential member of a cause or organisation, it's important to consider what unique skills, experiences, and qualities you can bring to the table. Although it's certainly important to be passionate about the cause and committed to its goals, it's also crucial to recognise and utilise your own strengths to contribute effectively.

One of the first things to consider is your personal skills and experiences. Do you have any special talents or expertise that could be useful to the cause? For example, perhaps you're a skilled writer and could contribute by creating compelling content for social media or the organisation's website. Or maybe you have experience in event planning and could help organise fundraisers or awareness campaigns. It's important to think about how your unique skills and experiences can be utilised in a way that helps the cause.

In addition to your personal skills and experiences, it's also important to consider your personality and character traits. What qualities do you bring to the table that could be beneficial to the cause? Are you a strong leader who can inspire and motivate others? Are you a good communicator and able to effectively convey the organisation's message? Do you have a strong sense of empathy and understanding of others' perspectives? These are all valuable qualities that can help make a difference in the cause.

Another aspect to consider is your network and connections. Do you have any relationships or connections that could be useful to the cause? Perhaps you know someone who works at a company that could donate resources or support the organisation financially. Or maybe you have connections in the media that could help raise awareness of the cause. Utilising your network and connections can be a powerful way to support the cause and make a difference.

Lastly, it's important to consider what you're willing and able to commit to in terms of time and resources. Although it's important to be passionate about the cause, it's also important to be realistic about what you can commit to. Are you able to dedicate a certain amount of time each week to volunteering or supporting the organisation in other ways? Do you have any financial resources you're able to contribute? It's important to be honest about your availability and resources so you can effectively contribute to the cause without overcommitting or burning out.

Overall, there are many different ways you can bring value to a cause or organisation serving humanity. By considering your unique skills, experiences, and personal qualities, as well as your network and connections and your ability to commit time and resources, you can effectively contribute to the cause and make a positive impact.

If you look around at some of the biggest charities and the faces who represent them, you'll find they bring many of their skills and talents to the cause. So ask yourself: what can you bring to the cause? Knowing this will help clarify your role in the bigger picture.

The Commitment Question

Are you willing to make a commitment? It's all well and good to have the time, resources, and skills, but if you don't have the dedication and determination, then nothing will come of it.

If your passion is helping the environment, for example, you need to be willing to commit to making small changes in your life. Do things like cutting down on waste or using reusable products, whenever possible. Commitment also means staying positive, even when progress is slow. All good causes take time and patience before they can be successful.

Bill and Melinda Gates and their foundation which is very well-known for their philanthropy and charity work, famously said, "If you are successful, it is because somewhere, sometime, someone gave you a life or an idea that started you in the right direction. Remember also that you are indebted to life until you help some less fortunate person, just as you were helped."

The bottom line is, that even if your passion doesn't lead to immediate results, the commitment will eventually pay off.

Boys Scout Motto sums this up:

On my honour I will do my best to do my duty to God and my country and to obey the Scout Law; To help other people at all times; To keep myself physically strong, mentally awake, and morally straight.

Your Understanding of the Cause

Finally, do you understand the cause? It's important to take the time to research and learn more about what inspired your passion in the first place. Learn as much as possible about how other people have made a difference and why they chose this particular route.

The one particular thing that sets a passionate person apart from others is their commitment to understanding the cause. They're deeply invested in learning the details and nuances of the issue and how best to solve it. That knowledge will be essential in crafting a meaningful plan of action that stands out among all the other causes. Consider your passion and commitment to helping as a social contract between you and the people you've chosen to assist, and that we all have a duty of care.

Prior to taking a plunge and starting your own charity, you should typically start with research. You need to understand the history, the impact of your work, and the people involved, especially their needs. That's why it's so important to research and educate yourself before you can move forward in making a difference.

Finding your passion is more than just understanding the cause; it's about feeling deeply committed to making a difference. It's not just about having the right skills and resources; it's also about having a strong desire to affect the world. Take your time to find what you're passionate about, research the cause, understand it, and then decide if you're in a position to make a difference. Once you have those pieces in place, the rest will fall into place, and your charity will be ready to take off!

Now, finding yourself is one part of the equation. The organisation you set up has to have some basic 'core values' or principles to help keep you on track. That's the next part of this journey in setting up your charity—understanding these fundamental principles.

Nothing in life is as rewarding as giving to a good cause. After all, charity is one of the cornerstones on which our society is built. However, there are some key principles an NGO or charity should adhere to for success.

The Seven Fundamental Principles of a Charity

These seven principles form the core of any charity, as per the Red Cross, and they must be respected and adhered to so you'll see lasting change and ensure the success of a charity.

Humanity

The principle of humanity is the most important one for charities. It requires we act with compassion and respect for everyone, regardless of differences in culture, race, gender, age, or belief system. We should always strive to ensure no one is forgotten and that everyone is given a fair chance at leading a good life.

For instance, every charity should have the factor of humanity and consider the duty of care in mind every time they make a decision. This means no one should be overlooked or ignored because of their financial status, age, gender, or any other factor.

Impartiality

Impartiality is the second principle of charity. It requires all decisions made by a charity to be based solely on need and not take into account any other factors such as religion, culture, or political affiliation. A charity should be impartial in its decision-making and ensure everyone who needs help is given the same treatment, regardless of their background.

The principle of impartiality is especially important in situations where resources are limited and many people are in need. This means decisions must be made based on who needs help most, rather than who's easiest to help or who has the most influence.

Voluntary Service

Voluntary service is a key principle of charity work. It requires all activities undertaken by a charity to be done without expectation of payment or reward. This encourages altruistic behaviour and helps ensure any donations given are used for their intended purpose, not for personal gain.

It also ensures charities remain independent from external influences such as politics or big businesses, which can sometimes have an agenda of their own. Charities must remain free from outside influence so they can continue doing what's best for their cause. This also means NGOs should resist becoming a rubber stamp for big businesses, who are often looking for charities that will help them clean up their images when there have been abuses to the environment or they have damaging human rights records.

Unity

The principle of unity is another important aspect of charity work. It requires all members of the charity, from volunteers to trustees, to be united in their vision and mission and act together as one team to promote the organisation's values and goals. This helps ensure everyone involved is clear about what needs to be done and how it should be achieved.

Universality

Although it sounds quite similar to humanity, the universality principle is different. This principle requires charities to recognise the needs and concerns of all people, regardless of their nationality or race.

This means charities must be willing to help anyone in need, no matter where they are from or what language they speak. It also encourages charities to think globally, rather than on a country-by-country basis, as well as to strive for global solutions to global problems.

Neutrality

The principle of neutrality is another important factor in charity work. This requires charities to never take sides or engage in political, religious, or military activities. This ensures charities remain independent and nonpartisan, so they can continue to do their work without fear of prejudice or bias from external sources.

Independence

The final principle of charity work is independence. This requires charities to strive to remain independent from any authority or power structure and be able to operate without fear of outside interference or influence. This is vital for the long-term success of a charity because it ensures they can continue to do their work without being constrained by external sources.

These are the core principles you must keep in mind when starting a charity.

The community or the society being served will only benefit if the charity is based on these principles. It's essential to be passionate and empathetic towards those in need while also understanding the importance of being impartial, voluntary, united, universal, neutral, and independent.

At the end of the day, you should remember charity work is not about monetary gains or seeking recognition, it's about helping people in need. Shun every suggestion or action that would manipulate or patronise the people your project is initiated to support. Development is a process; it takes time for people to change from the way they have been, hence patience and adopting/adapting the right implementation method is pertinent.

It's important to also view your project and set your lofty goals with the understanding that, no matter how powerful and impactful a charity may be, it can and should never think it will replace the government of the country it operates.

If you can keep this at the forefront of your mind when starting a charity, then you'll succeed in making a real difference in someone's life.

Key Takeaways

- *Passion is a strong emotion that drives you to make a difference.*
- *You need the time, resources, and skills to make a difference.*
- *Have commitment and determination to ensure success.*
- *Research and educate yourself on the cause before taking any action.*
- *Understand the core principles of charity work: humanity, impartiality, voluntary service, unity, universality, neutrality, and independence.*
- *Remember charity work is about helping people in need, not gaining money or recognition.*
- *Start by exploring your interests and hobbies. What activities do you enjoy doing in your free time? What subjects or topics do you enjoy learning about?*
- *Consider your values and what's important to you. What do you care about deeply and want to make a difference in?*
- *Seek out opportunities to try new things and gain new experiences. This can help you discover new passions and interests.*
- *Reflect on your past experiences and accomplishments. What have you excelled at or enjoyed doing in the past?*
- *Don't be afraid to take risks and pursue your passions, even if they may not be traditional or conventional.*

- *Seek guidance and support from friends, family, and mentors. They can provide valuable perspective and advice on finding your passion.*
- *Remember your passions may change and evolve over time, and it's okay to explore and pursue multiple passions. The important thing is to find something that brings you joy and fulfilment.*
- *Consider your commitment a social contract—and recognition or an award (if it comes) is merely the icing on the cake.*

Chapter 2
Getting Started

Knowledge is always the precursor to action, and that's certainly true when it comes to charity work. Before you can decide which type of organisation you want to get involved in, you need to understand the different types that exist and what they do. Organisations vary widely in their scope, purpose, and even how they're structured.

The first step is finding out what kind of organisation would fit your ideas, values, and goals. Here's an overview of some of the most common types of charities:

1. *Community-based organisations*: These are local charities that address specific needs within a given community or city. They may serve vulnerable populations such as children or seniors, provide essential services like food banks or shelters, or act as advocacy groups for a particular cause.
2. *National and international organisations*: These charities have a wider scope and reach, addressing global issues such as poverty, hunger, and climate change. They may be based in specific countries or operate across multiple countries.
3. *Religious organisations*: These charities come from various religious backgrounds, including Christianity, Judaism, Islam, Buddhism, Hinduism, and others. They usually focus on helping those in need within those faith communities or providing spiritual guidance and support to their members.

4. *Single-issue organisations*: These charities focus on a single issue such as animal welfare or environmental protection. They often have an advocacy component to their mission, in addition to providing direct services for those affected by the issue.
5. *Social service organisations*: These charities provide social services such as counselling, job training, and housing to people in need.

By understanding the different types of charities, you can narrow down your options and decide which is right for you. Before you start, research each organisation thoroughly so you know how it operates, as well as what its ideals are.

This will help to ensure that your involvement with a charity aligns with your values and goals. You may even find more than one type of organisation appeals to you—if so, there's nothing wrong with getting involved in multiple charities!

The best way to truly understand what kind of charity work you want is by getting hands-on experience. Volunteer your time at a local charity or participate in an event hosted by a national organisation. This will allow you to see firsthand how these organisations operate and what they do so you can make an educated decision about which one is right for you.

At times, we see many organisations merge and collaborate with one another to create synergies and better serve those in need. There are upsides and downsides to this approach. Let's take a detailed look at this.

Benefits

- *Leverage your resources*: By partnering with an existing organisation, you can leverage their resources and network to further your cause.
- *Save time and money*: When you join forces with a charity that already exists, you don't have to start from scratch to set up infrastructure or recruit volunteers. This can save a lot of time and money in the long run.
- *Build relationships*: Joining forces with other charities allows you to build relationships with people who share your values and goals.

Drawbacks

- *Loss of control*: Once you partner up with another organisation, some decisions may be out of your hands. This can lead to disputes and disagreements if there's a clash of ideologies.
- *Loss of autonomy*: When you merge with another organisation, it can be hard to maintain your identity and goals. This might mean compromising or sacrificing some aspects of your mission for the partnership to work.

Joining forces with existing charities can effectively expand your reach and have a greater impact on people in need. However, it is important to assess the risks and benefits before taking this approach to deciding which path is best for you and your cause.

Considering different charities and organisations, remember each has a unique culture, values, and mission. It's important to explore these options and find the one that best meets your needs.

The Different Types of Work Charities Do

Now, what kind of work do you want your charity to do? This is an incredibly important decision that can determine the type of organisation you create, how much funding and support you'll need, and even where you'll find volunteers.

There are many options for charities. These can be divided into direct impact and indirect impact.

Direct-Impact Organisations

The Red Cross, Salvation Army, Feeding America, or similar organisations focus on providing direct services. This can include anything from running a food pantry to giving out blankets and coats in the winter. These types of organisations usually have an immediate, tangible result; people can see the difference being made with their own eyes.

A direct-impact organisation usually has four key traits:

1. They provide direct services to those in need.
2. The services provided are immediate and tangible.
3. These organisations depend heavily on volunteers, donations, and other forms of support for their operations.

4. They tend to have a particular focus—such as hunger relief or homeless assistance—rather than trying to cover all social issues simultaneously.

Indirect Impact Organisations

Indirect impact organisations usually focus on advocacy and awareness-raising campaigns, educational initiatives, or research and development projects designed to create lasting change in society over time, rather than immediate solutions for individual needs. Greenpeace is an example of this type of organisation because it looks at global environmental issues such as climate change, deforestation, ocean pollution, and more.

These types of organisations usually have four key traits:

1. They focus on long-term systemic changes, rather than immediate solutions to individual needs.
2. They may also use lobbying or other forms of political activism to influence public policy in their favour.
3. These organisations depend heavily on volunteers, donations, and other forms of support for their operations, as well as knowledgeable professionals with expertise in the relevant fields.
4. They tend to have broader coverage—addressing multiple social issues simultaneously—rather than a particular focus like direct-impact organisations.

Let's dive deeper into some common types of organisations and what they do.

Direct service organisations provide a range of direct services, such as food banks, health clinics, homeless shelters, housing assistance programs, and more. Depending on their mission statement, they often have one or two core services but may also offer additional ones.

Advocacy organisations address social issues by raising awareness and lobbying for change at local, state, or national levels. These organisations usually have research teams that analyse societal trends to develop advocacy work strategies and are often partnered with other nonprofits with similar goals.

Education organisations focus on providing resources to individuals to give them the skills necessary to succeed in life. This includes anything from teaching financial literacy to offering GED classes and more.

Research and development organisations focus on researching and developing new solutions for social issues. These could include anything from drug research companies to think tanks focusing on economic reform or poverty reduction.

The Different Types of Work Charities Do

Charities are organisations that work to improve the lives of those in need. They provide support to those who are vulnerable and disadvantaged, as well as raising awareness of social issues and tackling them through campaigning and advocacy. But what types of work do charities actually do? In this section, we'll take a look at some of the different types of work charities undertake, including direct provision, campaigning and policy development, fundraising, research, and more. We'll discuss how these activities help bring about substantial positive changes in society, enabling us to create a better future for everyone.

What are the Different Types of Charities?

There are many different types of charities, all of which do important work to help those in need. Some of the most common types of charities include the following:

-Animal protection charities: These organisations work to rescue and care for animals, as well as promote animal welfare.

-Children's charities: These charities focus on helping children in need, whether it be through providing food and clothing or education and enrichment programs.

-Disaster relief charities: These organisations provide assistance to those who've been affected by natural disasters or other catastrophic events.

-Environmental charities: These groups work to protect the environment and promote sustainability.

-Health charities: These organisations work to improve the health and well-being of people around the world.

-Human rights charities: These groups work to defend and advance the rights of all people.

No matter what type of charity you choose to support, you can be sure your donation will be put to good use!

How Do Charities Help People?

Charities are organisations that exist to provide assistance and support to those in need. They can take many forms, including foundations, nonprofit organisations, and religious or community groups. Charities can provide a wide range of services, including financial assistance, medical care, education, housing, and other forms of support.

One of the primary ways charities help people is by providing financial assistance. This can take the form of direct financial support, such as grants or loans, or it can involve helping people access government benefits or other forms of assistance. Charities may also provide assistance with items like rent, utility bills, or groceries.

Another way charities help people is by providing access to education and training. This can involve helping people afford tuition for college or trade school, providing tutoring or other educational support, or offering job training and employment assistance.

Charities may also provide medical care and support to those in need. This can include providing access to medical treatment, prescription medications, and other forms of healthcare. Many charities also offer support for those dealing with mental health issues, addiction, or other challenges.

In addition to these services, charities may also provide housing assistance and support for those experiencing homelessness or living in substandard housing. This can include providing temporary shelter, helping people find permanent housing, or making repairs and improvements to existing housing.

Another important way charities help people is by providing emotional support and a sense of community. Many charities offer support groups, counselling, and other forms of social and emotional support to those in need. This can be especially important for those who may be isolated or feeling alone, and it can help people cope with challenges and adversity.

Overall, charities play a vital role in helping people in need and making a positive impact on communities. They provide a wide range of services and support to those who may be struggling, and they can aid in making a real difference in the lives of those they serve.

There are many ways in which charities help people. They can provide financial assistance, food, clothing, and other necessities to those who are struggling. They can also offer programs and services that help people improve their lives and get back on their feet.

Charities often work with other organisations to make sure people in need have access to the resources they need. They also lobby for changes in policy that will help the most vulnerable members of society. They also raise awareness about the issues affecting the lives of those they serve. The work of charities is thus essential to improving the lives of people in need and making our world a better place.

What are Some of the Most Popular Charities?

There are charities for just about everything these days. Some of the most popular charities include those that focus on animal welfare, children's causes, medical research, and environmental protection. No matter what your passion is, there's likely a charity out there that aligns with your values.

Donating to charity is a great way to give back to the community and make a difference in the world, but it's also important to do your research before giving your hard-earned money to any organisation. Make sure you understand how the charity will use your donations and what impact it will have before you write that check or click that 'donate' button.

There are many popular charities that work to address a wide range of issues and causes. Some of the most well-known and highly regarded charities include the following:

The Red Cross is a humanitarian organisation that provides emergency assistance, disaster relief, and disaster preparedness education in the United States and around the world.

UNICEF is a UN agency that works to protect the rights of children and promote their well-being. It operates in more than a hundred and ninety countries and territories, providing aid in the form of education, healthcare, sanitation, therapeutic feeding, and other services of critical importance to people in need.

The Salvation Army is a Christian organisation that provides a wide range of services to those in need, including emergency shelter, food assistance, and disaster relief.

World Vision is a Christian humanitarian organisation that works to improve the lives of children and their communities in the developing world. It operates in nearly a hundred countries and focuses on issues such as poverty, hunger, and disease.

Islamic Relief worldwide is a faith-inspired humanitarian and development agency working to save and transform the lives of some of the world's most vulnerable through four hundred and twenty-seven emergency projects in thirty-two countries.

Doctors Without Borders (Médecins Sans Frontières) is a humanitarian organisation that provides medical assistance to people in crisis situations, including conflict zones, natural disasters, and epidemics.

The Make-A-Wish Foundation is a charity that grants wishes to children with life-threatening medical conditions. It operates in more than fifty countries around the world.

Concern Worldwide operates in twenty-five of the world's poorest countries, helping people to achieve major and long-lasting improvements in their lives.

St. Jude Children's Research Hospital is a paediatric treatment and research facility that focuses on childhood cancer and other life-threatening diseases. It's known for its pioneering research and innovative treatments.

The Humane Society of the United States is an animal protection organisation that works to prevent animal cruelty and promote the humane treatment of animals. It operates a number of programs and initiatives, including animal rescue and rehabilitation, spay/neuter services, and animal advocacy.

The American Cancer Society is a nonprofit organisation that works to prevent cancer and support those affected by the disease. It operates a number of programs and initiatives, including cancer research, patient support services, and public education and awareness campaigns.

Habitat for Humanity is a nonprofit organisation that works to provide affordable housing for low-income families around the world. It operates through a network of local affiliates and relies on volunteers to build and repair homes for those in need.

These are just a few examples of the many charities that work to address a wide range of issues and causes. There are countless other organisations doing important work to make the world a better place, and there are many ways to get involved and support their efforts.

How Can I Start My Own Charity?

There are a number of ways to get started with your own charity. The first step is finding a cause you're passionate about. Once you have a focus, you can mobilise the savings you wish to use. This could be from a percentage of profits from your investment, reaching out and gathering support from your family foundation, starting a fundraiser, and or looking for sponsors. Register your charity as a nonprofit organisation to formalise it. This will provide tax benefits and make sure your finances are in order. Finally, start promoting your charity and get involved in the community to make a difference.

As we've seen, charities do a wide range of interventions to help people in need, ranging from providing food and shelter for the homeless to helping people find jobs or access education and water. Charities play an important role in society. A number of charities are first responders following the outbreak of war or major natural disasters. They are among the first to arrive and often the last to leave. These charities provide lifesaving services such as drinking water, food, shelter, and essential medical care.

We saw this in Nepal, Sierra Leone, Liberia, Yemen, South Sudan, Somalia, Ethiopia, Nigeria, and Ukraine, among others.

The next time you're looking for ways to give back and make a difference, consider donating your time or money to a charity that specialises in one of these areas. This will ensure your contributions are making an impact on someone's life and helping them reach their full potential and that your dime is accounted for. The point to note here is that, if you choose to start or run a charity, it is a serious business because the recipients depend on your donations and support, which could be the last straw they're holding on to.

Charities and charity work are way more important and serious than a lot of people think. Although there is room for one-off support to a course, however, we have also seen people floating or involved in charities mainly as 'humanitarian tourists', with a deep-seated interest only in being seen to do good. The point we are trying to make here is that there's a need for a strong vision, mission, and a solid commitment when you move to set up a charity.

Now that you understand the different types of organisations, it's time to decide what kind of charity you want to start!

It All Starts with Goals

Before you start a charity, it's important to define your mission and goals. Ask yourself: What type of work do I want to do? How will this work benefit society? Who are my target beneficiaries?

Doctors Without Borders (Médecins Sans Frontières), for example, focuses on providing medical and healthcare services to people in conflict zones. Greenpeace is dedicated to protecting the environment through campaigns, lobbying, and other advocacy initiatives. What does your charity aim to accomplish?

You should also consider what type of impact you want your charity to have. Do you want an organisation that provides direct services to beneficiaries or that works more systematically collaborating with others to make a greater impact? Will your charity focus on a single issue or multiple ones?

Once you've decided what kind of work you want, it's time to start researching organisations that align with your goals. Look for organisations with similar missions and values to yours and see how they're structured and operate. This will give you valuable insights into how to structure your own charity. It helps to start small, well focused and with a smaller geographical scope, learn, perfect your strategies and then grow over time.

You should also consider the legal aspects of setting up a charity. Depending on what country you're in, there could be different requirements for charitable organisations. It's important to research and understand these laws to ensure your organisation follows all the necessary regulations and keeps its nonprofit status.

We'll discuss these two topics in the next couple of chapters: how to structure your organisation and comply with the legal requirements and how to create a strategic plan for your charity.

In summary, getting started on a charity requires careful planning and research. Begin by establishing your goals and researching other organisations similar to what you'd like to create.

All charities, regardless of their sizes, have a clear vision and mission statement. You'll need to have your own too. The following are a few from established charities to guide your own:

Save the Children: Save the Children's vision is a world in which every child has the right to survival, protection, development, and participation. Its mission is to inspire breakthroughs in the way the world treats children and to achieve immediate and lasting change in their lives.

OXFAM: OXFAM's vision is a just and sustainable world, a world where people and the planet are at the centre of our economy, where women and girls live free from violence and discrimination, where the climate crisis is contained, and where governance systems are inclusive and allow for those in power to be held to account.

Concern Worldwide: Concern Worldwide dreams of a world where no one lives in poverty, fear, or oppression, where all have access to a decent standard of living and the opportunities and choices essential to a long, healthy, and creative life, a world where everyone is treated with dignity and respect.

Its mission is to help people living in extreme poverty achieve major improvements in their lives, which last and spread without ongoing support from Concern. To achieve this mission, it engages in long-term development work, builds resilience, responds to emergency situations, and seeks to address the root causes of poverty through our development education and advocacy work.

Next, we'll look into the legal aspects of setting up a charitable organisation to ensure everything is in compliance with the necessary regulations. With this knowledge, you're now ready to start forming your very own charity!

There are recognised global goals through which the United Nations and stakeholders articulate the needs of people and communities around the world. This is written up and known as the Sustainable Development Goals. It's also referred to as the 2030 Agenda to end poverty, protect the planet, and ensure prosperity for all. There are seventeen goals and each has its set targets. The goals are listed below:

- Goal 1. End poverty in all its forms everywhere.
- Goal 2. End hunger, achieve food security and improved nutrition, and promote sustainable agriculture.
- Goal 3. Ensure healthy lives and promote well-being for all at all ages.
- Goal 4. Ensure inclusive and equitable quality education and promote lifelong learning opportunities for all.
- Goal 5. Achieve gender equality and empower all women and girls.
- Goal 6. Ensure availability and the sustainable management of water and sanitation for all.
- Goal 7. Ensure access to affordable, reliable, sustainable, and modern energy for all.
- Goal 8. Promote sustained, inclusive, and sustainable economic growth, full and productive employment, and decent work for all.
- Goal 9. Build resilient infrastructure, promote inclusive and sustainable industrialisation, and foster innovation.
- Goal 10. Reduce inequality within and among countries.
- Goal 11. Make cities and human settlements inclusive, safe, resilient, and sustainable.
- Goal 12. Ensure sustainable consumption and production patterns.

- Goal 13. Take urgent action to combat climate change and its impacts.*
- Goal 14. Conserve and sustainably use the oceans, seas, and marine resources for sustainable development.
- Goal 15. Protect, restore, and promote sustainable use of terrestrial ecosystems, sustainably manage forests, combat desertification, and halt and reverse land degradation and halt biodiversity loss.
- Goal 16. Promote peaceful and inclusive societies for sustainable development, provide access to justice for all, and build effective, accountable, and inclusive institutions at all levels.
- Goal 17. Strengthen the means of implementation and revitalise the global partnership for sustainable development.

If you're starting your charity or funding a project, this list provides you with areas to consider for your focus.

Key Takeaways

- *Before you start, research the different types of charities to narrow down your options and decide which one is right for you.*
- *Get hands-on experience by volunteering your time at a local charity or participating in an event hosted by a national organisation.*
- *Organisations can merge and collaborate with one another to create synergies and better serve those in need—consider the pros and cons of this approach before committing.*
- *Each charity has a unique culture, values, and mission—choose the one that aligns with your own.*
- *Direct service organisations provide immediate and tangible solutions for people in need.*
- *Indirect impact organisations focus on advocacy, awareness-raising campaigns, educational initiatives, or research and development projects designed to create lasting change in society over time, rather than immediate solutions for individual needs.*
- *Knowing your goals and direction is crucial for getting started on a charity, as is understanding the legal aspects of setting up a charitable organisation.*

- *With research and hard work, you can create your own meaningful and effective charity!*
- *Charities are serious entities that require a solid vision and strong commitment.*

Chapter 3
Legally Establishing Your Charity

Establishing the legality of your charity can be a daunting process but it doesn't have to be. With the right information and guidance, you can establish your charity quickly and efficiently by following the necessary steps.

These steps will vary from country to country, but regardless of where you are in the world, there are a few key steps to take to establish your charity legally. We'll take the US and UK systems as examples and discuss the specifics of how to incorporate, obtain tax-exempt status, and register with the proper government agencies.

The Frameworks

A charity can have various shapes, sizes, and forms, but there are three main legal frameworks to decide between:

- *A nonprofit*: A charity that's organised as a nonprofit is an organisation that intends to use its profits for charitable activities. This type of charity must be incorporated in the jurisdiction where it operates and will have separate legal standing from its members. The nonprofit framework is common in the United States and the United Kingdom but may differ elsewhere.
- *A charitable trust*: A charitable trust is typically used when a single individual or family wants to establish a charity. It can be created under either wills or trusts law, which grants trustees control over assets held in trust on behalf of beneficiaries (i.e., the people who benefit from the

trust). Charitable trusts are more commonly used in the UK than in other countries.

- *A private foundation*: A private foundation is a non-exempt charitable organisation that has its own governing board but which relies on donations and grants to fund its activities. Private foundations are mostly seen in the United States, although they can also be established in other countries.

The Legal Structures Explained

Charities in the United States and the United Kingdom are typically set up as nonprofit organisations. In the United Kingdom, this is done through either a charitable trust or an incorporated limited liability company (CIC). Visit the Charity Commission's website. Verify your eligibility, appoint trustees, decide on your charity's structure, select a name, determine and articulate your charity's objectives, draft a governing document, ensure you meet the 'public benefit requirement', and obtain your registration certificate. Additionally, you will need to submit your bank or building society details, most recent accounts, contact details, postal address, trustees' names, dates of birth, and contact details, along with a copy of your charity's governing document (in PDF format).

You can register your charity in the United States as a 501(c)(3) organisation.

Charitable trusts allow two parties to put forward an agreement that sets out the purpose of the charity and how trustees will manage it. Trusts have fewer requirements than other structures but still provide protections for those running them from personal liability when it comes to debts or obligations.

An incorporated CIC means your charity is registered with Companies House in England and Wales. This gives you legal status as a separate entity from members and directors, and directors are protected from personal liability for the charity's debts.

In the United States, registering your charity as a 501(c) nonprofit organisation is a bit more complex than in the United Kingdom. The process involves filing Form 1023—Application for Recognition of Exemption with the Internal Revenue Service (IRS). This form requires detailed information about your charity's goals, activities, governance structure, and finances. It also requires documents such as financial statements and incorporation articles related to your charity's formation. Once the IRS approves, you'll be eligible to receive tax-exempt status and begin fundraising activities.

To be tax-exempt in the United States and the United Kingdom, you must meet certain rules and regulations. The primary rule is that proceeds from your charity's activities must be used for exclusively charitable purposes.

After establishing legal status in either country, it's important to register with all the appropriate government agencies. This could include registering for the Value Added Tax (VAT) in the United Kingdom or obtaining a Federal Employer Identification Number (FEIN) in the United States.

In the European Union, charities must register with the Charity Commission in each EU country. The process and requirements vary from member state to member state, so be sure to research the specific regulations for each country you plan to operate in.

Incorporation

Incorporating a charity involves filing the necessary paperwork in the jurisdiction where you plan to operate. After submitting the required forms, you'll receive documents confirming your charity's legal existence and recognising it as an independent entity from members or directors.

In a step-by-step way, the following is necessary to establish your charity legally:

- Define the purpose of your charity and write a mission statement.
- Research and select the appropriate legal structure for your charity.
- File for incorporation in the jurisdiction where you plan to operate.
- Apply for tax-exempt status in the United States or United Kingdom by filing Form 1023 with the IRS or registering with HMRC, respectively.
- Register with all appropriate government agencies such as obtaining a FEIN or VAT number, depending on which country you're operating in.
- Draft governing documents such as articles of association and policies and procedures that comply with applicable laws, regulations, and industry best practices.
- Develop a fundraising strategy and processes.
- Secure necessary insurance and other protections for your charity's directors, employees, volunteers, and beneficiaries.

Your charity's mission statement should be updated regularly to ensure it reflects the goals and objectives of your organisation.

Key Documents

To legally establish your charity, you need to produce several key documents. These include the following:

- *Articles of association*: This document sets out the purpose and structure of your charity and how its trustees manage it.
- *Memorandum of understanding (MOU)*: This document outlines the agreement between two or more parties who will collaborate on a project or activity related to the charity's mission statement.
- *Constitution/By-Laws*: This document outlines the charitable objectives and rules for running your organisation. It also states the rights and responsibilities of members, trustees, officers, and other stakeholders about your charity's activities.
- *Policies and procedures manual*: This manual serves as a guide for your charity, outlining the processes, procedures, and standards to be followed by staff and volunteers.

The above documents should be kept up-to-date with current legislation and regulations as they change from time to time.

The Team

Legally, your charity needs to have at least one director responsible for overseeing all activities. The directors should be experienced in running a charity and adhere to good governance and financial oversight principles.

Good governance practices include the following:

1. *Establishing a board of trustees with diverse skills and backgrounds to oversee the charity's operations.*
2. *Setting clear objectives for all activities undertaken by the charity.*
3. *Adopting an equitable recruitment process for staff and volunteers and ensuring they have appropriate training.*
4. *Ensuring sound financial management, including budgeting, accounting, and reporting processes that are regularly reviewed and updated as needed.*

5. *Developing effective internal communications systems among staff members, trustees, volunteers, advisors, and other stakeholders to ensure key messages reach those who need them quickly and accurately.*
6. *Taking responsibility for any legal issues arising from your charity's activities or decisions made by staff or trustees and ensuring appropriate steps are taken to resolve any issues.*

You'll also need to appoint trustees who provide independent advice and guidance on the charity's operations. Trustees are responsible for making decisions in their area of expertise and ensuring your charity's resources are managed responsibly. It is a legal requirement in nearly all countries where NGOs operate.

Professional Help

The legal process of establishing a charity can be complex and time-consuming. It's important to seek advice from qualified professionals such as lawyers, accountants, and financial advisors who understand your jurisdiction's legislation and have experience setting up 501(c) organisations or charities registered with HMRC in the United Kingdom.

The professionals best suited for this type of work will be familiar with the laws, regulations, and industry best practices that affect your charity. They can help you navigate the incorporation process, file for tax-exempt status, register your organisation with government agencies, and create the necessary documents for your charity's operations.

Establishing a charity is a complex process that requires careful planning and attention to detail. It's important to ensure your charity complies with applicable laws, regulations, and industry best practices. You should also recruit experienced trustees who understand good governance principles and are committed to protecting the organisations', and its beneficiaries', best interests. Finally, it's essential to seek legal advice from qualified professionals to ensure you've taken all the necessary steps to establish your charity and comply with applicable regulations legally.

Starting a charity is more than just having good intentions. You need to make sure your charity is legally established and compliant with the law. This involves filing applications, complying with regulations, and understanding the legal aspects of running a nonprofit organisation. But don't let that discourage you! Let's walk you through everything you need to know about legally establishing your charity. From understanding state laws to filing for tax exemption, get ready to dive into the nitty-gritty of setting up your charitable organisation in no time.

The Process of Legally Establishing Your Charity

The process of legally establishing your charity can be a complex and time-consuming process but it's essential if you want your organisation to be recognised as a legitimate charitable entity. The following are the steps you need to take to legally establish your charity, including registering your organisation, obtaining tax-exempt status, and complying with state and federal regulations:

Step 1: Choose a Legal Structure

The first step in legally establishing your charity is choosing the appropriate legal structure for your organisation. The most common options for charitable organisations are a nonprofit corporation or a charitable trust.

A nonprofit corporation is a legal entity that's formed to carry out a charitable purpose, such as advancing education or promoting health. Nonprofit corporations are typically governed by a board of directors and are required to file articles of incorporation with the state in which they're formed.

A charitable trust is a legal arrangement in which property or assets are held by one party (the trustee) for the benefit of another party (the beneficiary). Charitable trusts are typically created by a written document known as a trust deed or declaration of trust.

Step 2: Register Your Organisation

Once you've chosen the appropriate legal structure for your charity, the next step is registering your organisation with the appropriate state and federal agencies.

At the state level, you'll need to file articles of incorporation or a trust deed with the appropriate state agency, such as the secretary of state or attorney general. In addition, you may need to register with other state agencies, such as the Department of Revenue or the Department of Charitable Organisations.

At the federal level, you'll need to obtain an Employer Identification Number (EIN) from the IRS. This is a unique nine-digit number used to identify your organisation for tax purposes. You can obtain an EIN online or by mail by completing Form SS-4, Application for Employer Identification Number.

Step 3: Obtain Tax-Exempt Status

Once you've registered your organisation, the next step is obtaining tax-exempt status. This is an important step because it allows your charity to be exempt from paying federal income tax and may also allow donors to claim a tax deduction for their contributions.

To obtain tax-exempt status, you'll need to file an application with the IRS. The most common application for charitable organisations is Form 1023, Application for Recognition of Exemption Under Section 501(c)(3) of the Internal Revenue Code.

This form requires detailed information about your organisation, including its purpose, activities, and financial information.

Once you've filed your application, the IRS will review it and determine whether your organisation meets the requirements for tax-exempt status. This process can take several months, and you may be required to provide additional information or documentation.

Step 4: Comply with State and Federal Regulations

Once you've obtained tax-exempt status, you'll need to comply with state and federal regulations to maintain your status.

At the federal level, you'll need to file an annual information return with the IRS, such as Form 990, Return of Organisation Exempt from Income Tax. This form requires information about your organisation's financial activities, including its income, expenses, and assets.

In addition, you'll need to comply with other federal regulations, such as those related to lobbying and political activities. Charitable organisations are generally prohibited from participating in any political campaign activities, and they may be subject to limits on their lobbying activities.

At the state level, you'll need to comply with state regulations, such as those related to charitable solicitations and fundraising. Many states require charitable organisations to register with the state and obtain a licence before commencing operations.

Before you can legally establish your charity, you need to decide on its structure and how it will be governed. There are a few different ways to go about this, so it's important to consult with an attorney or accountant to get started. Once you've decided on the structure of your charity, you'll need to file the appropriate paperwork with the state in which it will be registered. This process can vary slightly from state to state, but it generally involves filing articles of incorporation and applying for tax-exempt status with the IRS. After your charity is legally established, you'll need to obtain a business licence and make sure all of your employees are properly trained.

The Benefits of Legally Establishing Your Charity

There are numerous benefits to legally establishing your charity, both for the organisation itself and for the individuals and communities it serves.

First and foremost, legally establishing your charity allows you to obtain tax-exempt status. This means donations made to the organisation are tax-deductible for the donors, which can be a major incentive for potential contributors. It also means the organisation itself is exempt from paying certain taxes, such as income and property tax. This can save the charity a significant amount of money that can then be redirected towards its mission and the people it serves.

In addition to tax benefits, legally establishing your charity also gives the organisation credibility and legitimacy. This can make it easier to attract donors and volunteers because people are more likely to trust and support organisations that have been formally recognised by the government. It can also make it easier to secure grants and partnerships with other organisations because they may be more willing to work with a legally established charity.

Another benefit of legally establishing your charity is the ability to form a board of directors. This group of individuals, who are elected by the organisation's members, is responsible for overseeing the management and operations of the charity. Having a board of directors can help ensure the organisation is being run in a responsible and transparent manner, and it can also provide valuable expertise and guidance to the organisation.

The legal establishment also allows charities to incorporate, which can provide some legal protections for members and directors. Incorporation means the organisation is recognised as a separate legal entity from its members and directors, which can provide some legal liability protection for them. This can be especially important for organisations that engage in activities that may involve some level of risk, such as working with vulnerable populations or providing services in dangerous or difficult environments.

Another benefit of legally establishing your charity is the ability to obtain insurance. Many insurance companies will not cover organisations that are not legally established, so this can be a crucial step in protecting the organisation and its members from potential liability. It can also be important in helping the organisation secure funding because many grants and partnerships may require the organisation to have insurance coverage.

In addition to the practical benefits mentioned above, legally establishing your charity can also help ensure the organisation is operating in accordance with the proper ethical and legal standards. This can be especially important for charities that work with vulnerable populations or handle sensitive information because it can help ensure the organisation is meeting its obligations to protect the people it serves and is upholding their rights.

Overall, legally establishing your charity can be a complex and time-consuming process but the benefits far outweigh the costs. By obtaining tax-exempt status, gaining credibility and legitimacy, forming a board of directors, and incorporating, and obtaining insurance, a legally established charity can be better equipped to achieve its mission and make a positive impact on the world.

When you legally establish your charity, you create a separate legal entity that can enter into contracts, own property, and engage in other business activities. This can insulate your personal assets from liability and help you attract more donors and volunteers.

There are many benefits to legally establishing your charity. First, it creates a separate legal entity that can enter into contracts, own property, and engage in other business activities. This can insulate your personal assets from liability. Second, it can help you attract more donors and volunteers. Third, it can make it easier to comply with government regulations. Fourth, it can give you the ability to apply for tax-exempt status.

Legally establishing your charity is an important step in ensuring your organisation is able to function effectively and pursue its goals. If you're considering starting a charity, be sure to consult with an experienced attorney who can help you navigate the process and ensure your organisation is properly established.

How to Get Started

If you want to establish a charity, there are a few things you need to do to make sure everything is done legally. First, you need to choose a name for your charity and make sure it's available as a legal entity. You'll also need to obtain any necessary licences and permits required by your state or local government. Once you have those things in place, you can start fundraising and accepting donations.

Establishing your charity legally can be a complicated process but it's necessary to ensure your organisation runs efficiently and ethically. Following the steps outlined will help you navigate the legal aspects of setting up a nonprofit organisation so you can make sure your mission has the greatest impact possible. With these tips in mind, we hope you're on track to successfully launch and manage a charitable organisation. Good luck!

The Process of Legally Establishing Your Charity

Establishing a charity can be a complex process but it can also be a rewarding one because it allows you to make a positive impact in your community or on a specific cause you're passionate about. Here's a general overview of the steps involved in legally establishing a charity:

Define your charitable mission: The first step in establishing a charity is to clearly define your mission and the purpose of your organisation. This will help guide your decision-making and ensure your charity is focused on a specific cause or group of people.

Choose a name for your charity: It's important to choose a name that's unique and reflects the mission and purpose of your organisation. You'll also want to ensure the name is not already in use by another charity.

Form a board of directors: A board of directors is responsible for the governance of your charity and makes important decisions about its direction and operation. It's important to assemble a diverse and committed board that can provide guidance and support to the charity.

Incorporate your charity: Incorporating your charity involves filing articles of incorporation with the state in which you plan to operate. This process can vary, depending on the state but it generally involves submitting a form and paying a fee. Incorporation provides legal protections for the directors and members of your charity.

Obtain federal tax-exempt status: To be recognised as a charitable organisation, you'll need to obtain tax-exempt status from the federal government. This involves applying for 501(c)(3) status with the IRS. The application process can be complex and may require the assistance of a lawyer.

Obtain state tax-exempt status: In addition to federal tax-exempt status, you may also need to obtain state tax-exempt status to be exempt from state taxes. The process for obtaining this status will vary, depending on the state in which you're located.

Create by-laws: By-laws are the rules and regulations that govern the operation of your charity. They outline the duties and responsibilities of the board of directors, the roles and powers of different board members, and the procedures for holding meetings and making decisions.

Hold an organisational meeting: Once you've completed the above steps, you'll need to hold an organisational meeting to adopt the by-laws and elect the initial board of directors. This meeting should be documented in the form of minutes.

Register with the state: Depending on the state in which you're located, you may need to register your charity with the state to solicit donations. This may involve filing additional paperwork and paying fees.

Obtain insurance: It's important to obtain insurance to protect your charity in the event of accidents or other liabilities. This may include general liability insurance, property insurance, and director and officer liability insurance.

Although the process of legally establishing a charity can be complex, it's an important step in ensuring your organisation is able to operate effectively and make a positive impact. It's advisable to seek the assistance of a lawyer or other professional to guide you through the process and ensure all the necessary steps are taken.

The process of legally establishing your charity can vary slightly from state to state, but there are some general steps you'll need to take. First, you'll need to choose a name for your charity and make sure it's available in your state. Next, you'll need to draft articles of incorporation and submit them to the appropriate state agency. Once your charity is incorporated, you'll need to obtain a tax-exempt status from the IRS. Lastly, you'll need to register with the state in which you plan to solicit donations.

What are the Benefits of Legally Establishing Your Charity?

Legally establishing your charity can provide numerous benefits to both the organisation and the individuals it serves. Here are some key advantages of taking this important step:

Legal protection: By legally establishing your charity, you're creating a legal entity that can enter into contracts, hold property, and sue or be sued in its own right. This legal protection can shield your organisation and its leaders from personal liability in the event something goes wrong.

Professionalism: Legally establishing your charity demonstrates a level of professionalism and commitment to your cause. It can also increase your credibility with donors, volunteers, and other stakeholders.

Access to funding: Many funders, including foundations and government grants, require organisations to be legally established before applying for funding. Without this status, you may miss out on valuable resources to support your work.

Tax-exempt status: In the United States, legally establishing your charity as a 501(c)(3) organisation allows you to qualify for tax-exempt status, which can save your organisation significant amounts of money on taxes. This can be especially beneficial if your organisation relies on donations to fund its operations.

Ability to accept donations: Legally establishing your charity allows you to accept donations and gifts without the donor having to worry about whether they're tax-deductible. This can make it easier to raise funds and support your mission.

Public accountability: Legally establishing your charity means you must follow certain rules and regulations, such as filing annual reports and adhering to financial transparency requirements. This helps ensure your organisation is accountable to the public and your funds are being used appropriately.

Long-term sustainability: Legally establishing your charity can help ensure your organisation is sustainable in the long term. This can be especially important if your organisation relies on donations or grants because these sources of funding can be unpredictable.

Better management: Legally establishing your charity can help you develop more structured and effective management practices, which can improve your organisation's efficiency and effectiveness. This can be especially important if your organisation is growing or expanding its operations.

Ability to hire staff: Legally establishing your charity allows you to hire staff, which can be essential if your organisation is expanding or if you need to bring in specialised expertise.

Increased impact: Legally establishing your charity can help you reach more people and make a bigger impact on your cause. This can be especially important if your organisation is working to address a complex issue or if you're serving a large and diverse community.

Overall, legally establishing your charity can provide numerous benefits that can help your organisation be more effective, sustainable, and impactful. Although the process of legally establishing your charity can be time-consuming and complex, the long-term benefits are well worth the effort.

There are many benefits to legally establishing your charity. First, it ensures your organisation is recognised as a 501(c)(3) by the IRS, which allows you to receive tax-deductible donations and grants. Additionally, it allows you to apply for government funding and contracts. Moreover, donors may feel more confident donating to a legally established charity because they can be sure their donation will go towards the charitable cause they intended. Finally, having a legal structure in place can help ensure your charity runs smoothly and efficiently.

How to Go About Legally Establishing Your Charity

Starting a charity can be a rewarding and fulfilling experience but it's important to ensure you follow the legal requirements for establishing a charity in your jurisdiction and in the country you intend to work. This process can vary, depending on where you're located, but there are some general steps you can follow to get started.

Determine your charitable purpose: The first step in establishing a charity is to define its purpose and determine whether it meets the legal definition of a charity. A charity is typically defined as a nonprofit organisation established for the purpose of promoting the common good and providing benefits to the public. Some common charitable purposes include relieving poverty, advancing education, promoting health, and protecting the environment.

Choose a name for your charity: Choose a unique and appropriate name for your charity that reflects its purpose and mission. You'll need to check with your local government to ensure the name you've chosen isn't already in use by another organisation and to see if there are any restrictions on the types of names that can be used for charities.

Incorporate your charity: The next step is to incorporate your charity as a legal entity. This will typically involve filing articles of incorporation with your state or local government and obtaining a corporate charter. Depending on your jurisdiction, you may also need to obtain tax-exempt status from the IRS to be eligible to receive tax-deductible donations.

Develop policies and by-laws: Once your charity is incorporated, you'll need to develop by-laws, which are the rules and regulations that govern how your organisation will be run. These should include provisions for how the board of directors will be elected, how meetings will be conducted, and how decisions will be made.

Appoint a board of directors: A charity is typically governed by a board of directors, which is responsible for making policy decisions and overseeing the organisation's operations. It's important to appoint a diverse and qualified board of directors who are committed to the charitable mission of the organisation.

Obtain any necessary licences and permits: Depending on the nature of your charity and the activities it will be engaged in, you may need to obtain various licences and permits to operate legally. For example, if your charity will be conducting fundraising events, you may need to obtain a special fundraising permit.

Register with the appropriate government agencies: To operate legally, your charity will need to register with the appropriate government agencies, such as the IRS and your state's charity regulator. This will typically involve filing various forms and documents and providing information about your organisation and its activities.

Establish financial controls: It's important to establish financial controls to ensure your charity is run in a transparent and accountable manner. This may involve setting up a system for tracking donations and expenses, establishing policies for handling financial transactions, and ensuring you have adequate insurance coverage.

By following these steps, you can ensure your charity is legally established and ready to carry out its charitable mission.

If you're interested in establishing a charity, there are a few things you need to do to make sure it's legal. First, you'll need to choose a name and purpose for your charity. Once you have that figured out, you'll need to get incorporation papers from your state and file them with the IRS. You'll also need to apply for 501(c)(3) status with the IRS, which will allow your donors to deduct their contributions from their taxes. Lastly, you'll need to create some governing documents for your charity, such as by-laws or articles of incorporation. Once you have all of these things in place, you can start soliciting donations and doing good work in your community!

By researching the legal requirements of establishing a charity, creating the necessary paperwork, and recruiting experienced trustees and advisors, you'll be well on your way to setting up a successful charity that meets its goals and serves its beneficiaries.

Key Takeaways

- *Charities in the United States and the United Kingdom are typically set up as nonprofit organisations.*
- *A charitable trust allows two parties to put forward an agreement that sets out the purpose of the charity and how trustees will manage it.*
- *In the United States, registering your charity as a 501(c)(3) organisation requires filing Form 1023 with the IRS and submitting detailed information about your charity's goals, activities, governance structure, and finances.*
- *To be tax-exempt in either country, proceeds from your charity's activities must be used exclusively for charitable purposes.*
- *Key documents are needed to legally establish your charity, including an Articles of Association, Memorandum of Understanding (MOU), Constitution, and Policies and Procedures Manual.*
- *In addition to the legal paperwork, you should recruit experienced trustees who understand good governance principles and are committed to protecting the organisation's and its beneficiaries' interests.*
- *Finally, it's essential to seek legal advice from qualified professionals to ensure all the necessary steps have been taken to establish your charity and comply with applicable regulations legally.*
- *Clearly define your organisation's mission, vision, and values. These serve as the foundation for all strategic planning decisions.*
- *Identify your organisation's strengths, weaknesses, opportunities, and threats. This helps you understand your current situation and what factors may affect your future success.*
- *Set clear, measurable, and achievable goals. These should be aligned with your mission and vision and should be specific, measurable, attainable, relevant, and time-bound.*

- *Develop a detailed action plan to achieve your goals. This should include the specific tasks, milestones, and deadlines for each goal.*
- *Assign responsibilities and resources to ensure the action plan is implemented effectively.*
- *Monitor and evaluate progress regularly. This allows you to make any necessary adjustments to the plan and ensure you're on track to achieve your goals.*
- *Communicate the strategic plan to all stakeholders. This ensures everyone is aware of the direction the organisation is headed, as well as their role in achieving its goals.*
- *Review and revise the plan periodically. As your organisation changes and evolves, your strategic plan should be updated to reflect these changes.*

Chapter 4
Creating a Strategic Plan

Strategic planning is an essential part of any business or organisation. It helps you align your goals with your resources and develop a road map for success. A good strategic plan will help you articulate your core objectives, prioritise tasks, and make adjustments, as needed. But how do you create a strategic plan? We'll go through the steps of creating a comprehensive strategy, from setting goals to measuring performance along the way. Let's get started!

The legal structure determines the security, growth, and sustainability of your charity. But what will you do once it's all in place? Put simply, you need a plan. A strategic plan is like a road map that helps you achieve your goals and objectives. It guides the direction of your charity, defines where you want to go, and provides an actionable strategy for getting there.

Start with clear objectives for your charity. In this chapter, we'll discuss the importance of setting SMART objectives and identifying your target audience, and we'll teach you how to create an action plan for achieving them.

Often, most enthusiasts starting out and running with their passion get quickly burnt out along the line when they cannot easily see the results of their investments. One classic mistake made is that their project is often not addressing a core need. Yes, there's poverty and there's hunger but often most newbies don't ask themselves the 'why'. Professionals alike also make these mistakes, so it's not too peculiar; however, it makes a world of difference when you understand the cause of the problem and use that knowledge to develop an intervention that addresses it. One of the most used tools by project management practitioners when brainstorming is the problem tree.

'Problem tree analysis (also called Situational analysis or just Problem analysis) helps to find solutions by mapping out the anatomy of cause and effect around an issue in a similar way to a mind map, but with more structure'. This tool interrogates the root causes of issues and places them in perspective, teasing out the cause and effect. An example of the problem tree is provided in the box below:

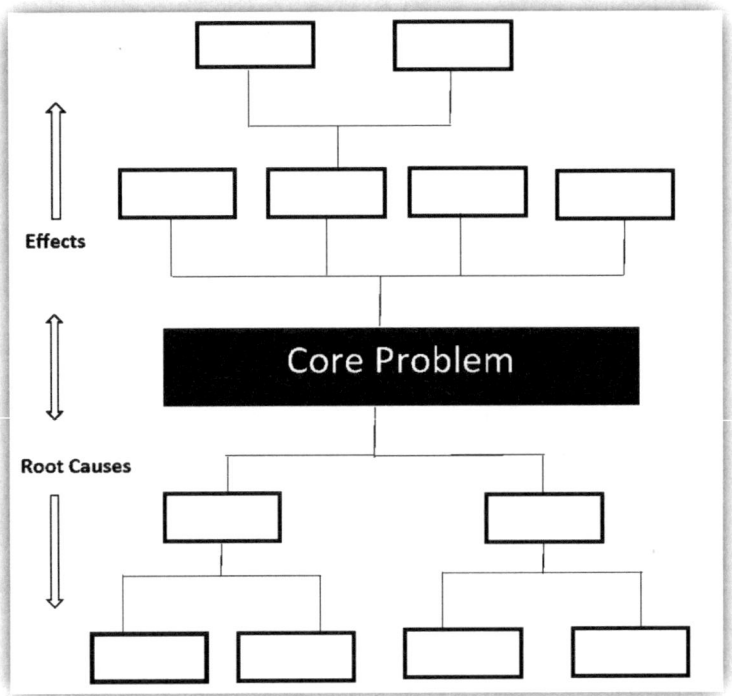

The MSP guide is useful in explaining how to go about doing Problem Tree Analysis, step by step.

Problem tree analysis is best carried out in a small focus group of about six to eight people using flip chart paper or overhead transparency. It is important that factors can be added as the conversation progresses.

Step 1: Discuss and agree on the problem or issue to be analysed. The problem can be broad, as the problem tree will help break it down. The problem or issue is written in the centre of the flip chart and becomes the 'trunk' of the tree. This becomes the 'focal problem'. The problem should be an actual issue everyone feels passionate about, described in general, keywording.

Step 2: Identify the causes of the focal problem—these become the roots—and then the consequences, which become the branches. These causes and consequences can be created on post-it notes or cards, perhaps individually or in pairs so that they can be arranged in a cause-and-effect logic.

The heart of the exercise is the discussion, debate, and dialogue generated in the process of creating the tree. Take time to allow people to explain their feelings and reasoning, and record related ideas and points that come up on separate flip chart paper under titles such as 'solutions', 'concerns' and 'dilemmas'.

What is a Strategic Plan?

A strategic plan is a document that sets out an organisation's goals, objectives, and strategies. It's a blueprint for how an organisation can achieve its goals and objectives over a set period of time.

The main purpose of a strategic plan is to ensure all members of an organisation are working towards the same goals. It also provides a framework for decision-making and can be used to measure progress and evaluate results.

Strategic planning usually takes place at the top level of an organisation, but it can also be done at the team or individual level. According to Balanced Scorecard Institute, "Strategic planning is an organisational management activity that is used to set priorities, focus energy and resources, strengthen operations, ensure that employees and other stakeholders are working towards common goals, establish agreement around intended outcomes/results, and assess and adjust the organisation's direction in response to a changing environment."

All strategic planning process usually begins with a review of the organisation's current situation, including its strengths, weaknesses, opportunities, and threats. Using brainstorming sessions and consultation as a tool, this is followed by setting goals and objectives and developing strategies to achieve them. The final step is to put the plan into action and monitor progress.

The Components of a Strategic Plan

As you create your strategic plan, there are several key components to keep in mind. A good strategic plan should include the following:

1. *A clear statement of your organisation's mission and vision.* Your mission statement is a brief description of what your organisation does,

whereas your vision statement is a longer-term view of where you want your organisation to be. Be sure to keep these statements concise and focused.

2. *An analysis of your current situation.* This includes an evaluation of both your internal strengths and weaknesses, as well as an examination of external opportunities and threats. This step will help you identify areas where you need to improve or make changes to achieve your desired future state.
3. *Goals and objectives.* Once you have a good understanding of where you are and where you want to be, it's time to set some specific goals and objectives that will help get you there. These should be specific, measurable, achievable, relevant, and time-bound (SMART).
4. *Strategies and action plans.* Now it's time to develop the strategies and action plans that will help you achieve your goals and objectives. These should be detailed enough that they can be implemented and monitored effectively.
5. *Budgeting and resource allocation.* To carry out your strategies and action plans, you'll need to allocate adequate resources (time, money, staff, etc.). This step ensures you have the necessary resources in place to make your plan a reality. It's also important to state the sources of your funds and the funding strategies you intend to adopt for the period of the strategic period.

Why is a Strategic Plan Important?

A strategic plan is important because it provides a road map for achieving business goals. It can help increase efficiency and productivity while also reducing costs. Additionally, a well-crafted strategic plan can improve communication and coordination between different departments and employees. By having a clear plan in place, businesses can better adapt to changes in the marketplace and make decisions in line with their overall objectives.

How to Create a Strategic Plan

There's no one-size-fits-all answer to creating a strategic plan, as the process will vary, depending on the specific organisation and its goals. However, there are some essential steps all organisations should take when creating strategic plans.

1. Define the organisation's mission, vision, and values. These are the foundation of the organisation and will guide all decision-making.
2. Conduct a situational analysis to assess the organisation's current strengths, weaknesses, opportunities, and threats. This information will help inform strategy development.
3. Set goals and objectives for the organisation. These should be SMART.
4. Develop strategies to achieve the goals and objectives. Strategies should be specific actions that will address the identified opportunities and threats while leveraging the organisation's strengths.
5. Create an implementation plan that outlines who's responsible for each task, when it should be completed, and how it will be carried out.
6. Monitor progress and periodically review and adjust the plan, as needed, to ensure it remains effective in achieving the organisation's goals.

Tips for Creating an Effective Strategic Plan

An effective strategic plan must be clear, concise, and actionable. It should also be achievable, relevant, and aligned with your company's mission and values. Here are some tips for creating an effective strategic plan:

1. Define your company's mission and vision.
2. Set realistic goals that are aligned with your company's mission and vision.
3. Develop strategies to achieve your goals.
4. Implement your plan and track progress.
5. Adjust your plan, as needed, based on results achieved.

A strategic plan is a great tool for businesses and charities to use to maximise their chances of success. Creating an effective strategic plan requires careful consideration and analysis of internal and external factors, as well as looking at the short- and long-term goals. The development process includes analysing data, setting objectives, creating action plans, and establishing benchmarks. Taking the time to develop a thoughtful strategy will ensure your business succeeds and grows over time.

The Components of a Strategic Plan

To put it simply, there are six key components to creating a strategic plan. We'll look at each in detail.

Theory of Change

If you've ever come across the term, 'Theory of Change', it's a tool that depicts the interconnectedness of your resources (input), output, outcomes and impact along with influencing factors. Theory of Change framework or illustration is useful to help you look at or put the wider impact of your charity into perspective. The process works on two key levels:

Firstly, you need to define the problem or issue your charity wants to address.

Secondly, you will identify the solutions and outcomes that need to take place in order for your target audience or beneficiaries to have their needs met. It's a great way of looking at how your charity can make an impact on its community.

The whole process works in a retrospective manner. Let's say the plan is to end homelessness in your community. This would be the long-term goal. The intermediary goals would be to create job opportunities and provide housing support and counselling services.

Once you've set your objectives, it's time to establish the key activities that will help you achieve them. This includes setting timelines for each of the tasks, developing a budget, and deciding how best to allocate resources.

SWOT Analysis

The second step or component of the strategic plan is to undertake an analysis of both factors external and internal to your organisation. To do this, SWOT is a popular analysis tool used by practitioners. SWOT stands for **S**trengths, **W**eaknesses, **O**pportunities, and **T**hreats. It's an analytical technique that helps you assess your charity's current position, identify areas of improvement, and develop strategies to achieve them. SWOT has remained a popular tool among humanitarian practitioners ever since it was introduced in the 1960s.

Let's take an example of a charity that wants to create an after-school program for children. A SWOT analysis of this particular program might look like this:

- *Strengths*: Quality teachers/established relationships with local schools and businesses
- *Weaknesses*: Limited resources and limited funding opportunities
- *Opportunities*: Increased access to grants and potential collaboration with other charities
- *Threats*: High demand for after-school programs in the community, as well as competition from other organisations.

By understanding your strengths and weaknesses, you can identify opportunities and threats. This will help you make informed decisions on how best to tackle them.

A SWOT analysis is one of the most effective and efficient ways to analyse your internal and external influences towards developing a strategic plan. The chart below was simplified by Valueprop to help you understand how to use the SWOT tool:

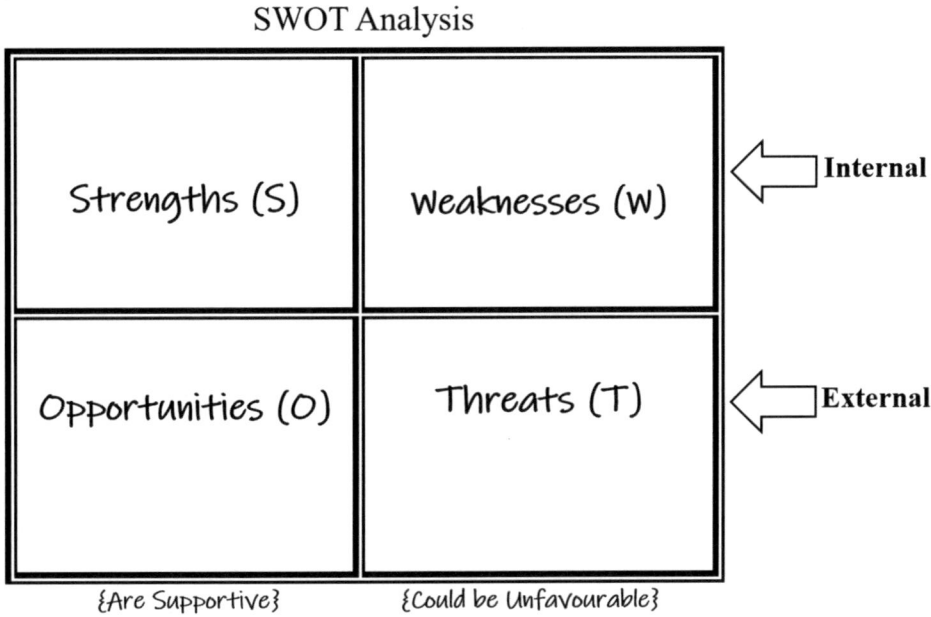

Figure 1: SWOT Analysis Table

Getting the Basics Sorted

The boring work often has the most impact. Once you have a clear goal, you'll need to establish the basics such as legal requirements, marketing strategies, and fundraising plans. You may also need to consider your charity's public relations efforts.

From the onset, having a blueprint of the necessary steps to achieve your goals will make it easier to plan, execute, and monitor progress. This can involve setting up a board of directors, developing an operational structure and policies, and creating a budget.

Setting Objectives for a Fixed Period

A strategic plan is only as good as its objectives. Your charity should set SMART objectives and achievable goals—that is, SMART goals. This will ensure your objectives are realistic and achievable within a fixed period of time. It's important to track progress against each goal so you can adjust plans accordingly.

A plan usually has a fixed time period. Let's say three to five years. It's important to understand the plan can change due to external factors such as economic conditions or political changes, so you may need to adjust your goals accordingly. To have proper objectives, choose the three most pressing needs of your target audience and create specific goals that address each need. This will help you focus on the areas where your charity can have the greatest impact.

A charity working towards clean water might aim to provide clean water to ten thousand people at the end of three years. This would be SMART because it's specific, measurable, achievable, realistic, and time-bound. The other two objectives might be to educate a fixed number of people about the importance of clean water and to raise a certain amount of funds.

Let's at this point measure the risk of over-simplifying the need to have well-thought-out logic. To help you work through this, the tool of choice for most big donors is one borrowed from the engineering field called the logical framework (or log frame). Imagine a log frame as a 4x4 table of logic. Below is an example of a log frame adapted for an EU-funded project (annex_c_e3d_logical_framework_en):

		Intervention logic	**Indicators**	**Sources and Means of Verification**	**Assumptions**
Overall objective: Impact		The broader, long-term change that will stem from the project and a number of interventions by other partners.	Measure the long-term change to which the project contributes. To be presented disaggregated by sex.	To be drawn from the partner's strategy.	
Specific Objectives:	**Outcomes**	The direct effects of the project that will be obtained in the medium term and which tend to focus on the changes in behaviour resulting from the project Outcome = Oc (Oc 1, Oc 2, etc.)	Measure the change in factors determining the outcomes. To be presented disaggregated by sex.	Sources of information and methods used to collect and report (including who and when/how frequently).	Factors outside the project management's control that may affect the outcome-impact linkage.

Outputs	The direct/tangible outputs (infrastructure, goods, and services) delivered by the project. Outcome = Oc Op 1.1. (related to Oc 1) Op 1.2. (related to	Measure the degree of delivery of the outputs. To be presented disaggregated by sex.	Idem as above for the corresponding indicator.	Factors outside project management's control that may affect the output-outcome linkage.
	Oc 1) (…) Op 2.1. (related to Oc 2) (…)			

Activities	What are the key activities to be carried out to produce the outputs? Group the activities by result and number them as follows: A 1.1.1.—'Title of activity' A 1.1.2.—'Title of activity' (related to Op 1.1.) A 1.2.1.—'Title of activity' (…) (related to Op 1.2.) A 2.1.2.—'Title of activity' (…) (related to Op 2.1.) Means What are the political, technical, financial, human and material resources required to implement these activities, e.g., staff, equipment, supplies, operational facilities, etc. Costs What are the action costs? How are they classified? (Breakdown in the Budget for the Action)

Adapted from the EU Grant Application Annex II: Logical Framework

Monitoring Progress Through Regular Assessments

You'll need to regularly review progress against objectives and make necessary adjustments along the way. This will help ensure you're on track and don't miss any opportunities that could benefit your charity.

Regular assessments are also a great way of holding yourself accountable for results. The key is to set up protocols that provide clear guidelines for monitoring progress. This could include weekly check-ins with team members, quarterly reviews with board members, and monthly reports outlining progress towards each milestone.

KPIs

The most effective monitoring tools are *key performance indicators*. A KPI is a metric that helps measure success against objectives. Some examples of KPIs for a charity include website visits, number of donors, and total funds raised. By tracking these metrics regularly, you can ensure you're on track to meet your goals.

OKRs

Another good monitoring tool is OKRs (objectives and key results). This involves setting clear objectives with a timeline, along with an associated set of measurable outcomes. For example, the objective could be to increase donations by twenty per cent, whereas the key result could be that you need to generate ten thousand new donors within six months.

It is an acceptable practice to set objectives, by simply turning the problems identified during your assessments/brainstorming sessions into an intention to make them right, correct the wrong or find an answer. The summary of all the problems becomes your overall objectives, and the independent problems become the specific objectives or outcomes/results as you will see later in the section on impact analysis and logical framework.

This type of system ensures everyone involved in the project understands what needs to be done and when it needs to be achieved.

Creating the Action Plan

The last strategic plan element is an action plan. This outlines the steps that need to be taken to achieve your objectives. It should include a timeline, the resources required, and the responsibilities assigned for each stage of the process.

An action plan helps ensure everyone involved knows what their role is and when they need to complete it. When creating an action plan, break down tasks into manageable chunks so you can keep track of your progress and make necessary adjustments along the way.

Creating a strategic plan is essential for any charity looking to reach its goals in a short amount of time. By setting SMART goals, monitoring progress through regular assessments, and creating an action plan with clear timelines and responsibilities, you'll be well on your way to achieving success.

The Importance of Target Audience

Knowing your target audience is absolutely essential when creating any strategic plan. Why? Because if you don't know who you're trying to reach, how can you successfully design a strategy to get there? A good rule of thumb when considering the target audience is the old adage, 'know thy customer'. They're the primary stakeholders. By knowing your target audience, you'll be able to identify your potential donors and supporters; it will also help determine the messaging that resonates best with them and the most effective channels they can reach.

An easy way to start building up an understanding of your target audience is by asking yourself questions such as the following: What are their interests? Why are they in this situation? Could they possibly be able to help themselves out of the situation? What challenges do they face in life? How can my charity provide unique solutions to those challenges? Doing so will give you a clearer idea of the type of people who'll be most interested in your charity and how to craft a message that resonates with them.

Once you understand your target audience, you can start crafting an action plan around how best to reach them. This could include anything from creating targeted email campaigns to actively engaging with potential supporters on social media. Whatever methods you choose, it's important to keep your messages concise and compelling because this is often the difference between success and failure in any outreach effort.

The importance of the target audience cannot be overstated. A target audience is a specific group of individuals that a business, organisation, or individual is trying to reach and influence through marketing efforts. Understanding and effectively targeting the right audience is crucial for the success of any marketing campaign.

There are several reasons why identifying and targeting a specific audience is so important. First and foremost, it allows marketers to tailor their message and marketing efforts to the specific needs and interests of the target audience. This helps ensure the marketing message will be more relevant and effective, leading to higher conversion rates and a more successful campaign overall.

Additionally, targeting a specific audience allows marketers to more efficiently allocate their resources. By focusing on a specific group of individuals, marketers can avoid wasting time and money on marketing efforts that may not be effective for more general audiences. This enables them to make the most out of their marketing budget and get the best return on investment.

Another important reason to target a specific audience is it helps to build and maintain brand loyalty. When a business consistently delivers marketing messages that are relevant and targeted to the needs and interests of its target audience, it can help build a strong, loyal customer base. This is especially important in today's competitive marketplace, where businesses need to work hard to stand out and differentiate themselves from the competition.

Furthermore, targeting a specific audience can help increase the overall impact and reach of a marketing campaign. By focusing on a specific group of individuals, marketers can more effectively target their marketing efforts and reach a larger number of potential customers. This can lead to increased brand awareness and, ultimately, increased sales and revenue.

However, it's important to note targeting a specific audience doesn't mean businesses should exclude other groups or individuals. Rather, it simply means the marketing efforts should be primarily focused on a specific group of individuals. This allows businesses to effectively reach and influence their target audience while still being open to attracting new customers from other groups.

So how can businesses effectively identify and target their target audience? There are several key steps businesses should follow to ensure they're targeting the right audience.

Define your target audience: The first step in targeting a specific audience is to clearly define who you're trying to reach. This should include details such as age, gender, income level, interests, and location.

Understand the needs and interests of your target audience: Once you have defined your target audience, it's important to understand what they're looking for and what their interests and needs are. This will help you tailor your marketing efforts to meet their specific needs and interests.

Use data and research to inform your targeting efforts: There are many different tools and resources available that can help businesses better understand and target their audience. This includes factors like customer surveys, focus groups, and market research.

Segment your target audience: Once you've defined and understood your target audience, it's important to segment them into smaller, more specific groups. This will allow you to tailor your marketing efforts to the specific needs and interests of each group.

Use targeted marketing efforts to reach your audience: Once you have identified and segmented your target audience, it's important to use targeted marketing efforts to reach them. This includes items like targeted social media ads, email marketing, and targeted content marketing.

In conclusion, the importance of targeting a specific audience cannot be overstated. By understanding and effectively targeting the right audience, businesses can increase the effectiveness of their marketing efforts, build brand loyalty, and ultimately drive increased sales and revenue. Therefore, it's crucial for businesses to take the time to carefully identify and target their audience to get the most out of their success.

Success and failure in any charity lie largely in how well it's managed. By creating a strategic plan that focuses on setting SMART goals, monitoring progress regularly, and understanding your target audience, you can ensure your hard work pays off. After all, the only way to reach success is by having a plan.

Key Takeaways

- *Creating a strategic plan is essential for any successful charity. A strategic plan provides a road map to help you achieve your goals and set SMART objectives.*
- *SWOT analyses help you assess your charity's current position and identify areas of improvement.*
- *Setting fixed objectives that are SMART will ensure your objectives are realistic and achievable within a time period.*
- *Regular assessments and tracking KPIs will help you stay on track towards your objectives.*
- *An action plan with clear timelines and responsibilities will help ensure everyone involved knows what they need to do and when it needs to be done.*
- *Knowing your target audience is essential to crafting a message that resonates with them and determining which channels are most effective for reaching out.*
- *Identifying your target audience is crucial for the success of your marketing efforts.*
- *Understanding your target audience helps you tailor your messaging to appeal to their specific needs and wants.*

- *Knowing your target audience allows you to create content that resonates with them and helps you choose the most effective channels for reaching your audience.*
- *Knowing your target audience allows you to segment your marketing efforts to more effectively reach different groups within your audience and helps you create more targeted and personalised marketing campaigns.*
- *Identifying your target audience can help you forecast future sales and revenue and identify new opportunities for product or service development.*
- *Knowing your target audience can help you make informed decisions about your brand positioning and allows you to create a more cohesive brand experience for your audience.*
- *Identifying your target audience helps you optimise your website and other marketing materials for maximum effectiveness.*
- *Understanding your target audience helps you create a more effective marketing budget and allocate resources appropriately.*

Chapter 5
Systems and Processes

Systems and processes are essential components of any organisation because they help ensure tasks are completed efficiently and effectively. A system is a set of interconnected elements that work together to achieve a common goal. Processes, in contrast, are the specific steps or actions taken within a system to accomplish a specific task or achieve a desired outcome (10). Together, systems and processes form the backbone of an organisation's operations and play a critical role in its success.

One of the key benefits of systems and processes is they provide a clear structure and framework for completing tasks. This helps ensure all necessary steps are taken and that tasks are completed in a consistent and predictable manner. For example, a sales process might include steps such as identifying potential customers, making initial contact, conducting a needs assessment, presenting a solution, and closing a sale. By following this process consistently, a sales team can increase its chances of success and make more effective use of its time and resources.

Another key benefit of systems and processes is they allow organisations to track and measure their performance. By establishing metrics and tracking data related to their systems and processes, organisations can identify areas where they're performing well and areas where they need to improve. This can help organisations identify bottlenecks or inefficiencies in their operations and make necessary changes to improve their performance.

There are several types of systems and processes that organisations may use. Some common examples include the following:

Business processes: These are the core processes that drive an organisation's operations, such as sales, marketing, production, and finance. Business processes are often supported by information systems and other tools to help automate and streamline their operations.

Management processes: These are the processes that help organisations plan, organise, and control their operations. Examples of management processes include budgeting, performance management, and strategic planning.

Project management processes: These are the processes that organisations use to plan, execute, and complete specific projects. Project management processes typically include steps such as defining the scope of the project, establishing a timeline, assigning tasks and responsibilities, and tracking progress.

Quality management processes: These are the processes organisations use to ensure their products or services meet the desired level of quality. Quality management processes often include steps such as setting quality standards, conducting inspections, and analysing data to identify areas for improvement.

Supply chain processes: These are the processes organisations use to manage the flow of goods and services from raw materials to the end consumer. Supply chain processes may include steps such as sourcing materials, production, transportation, and distribution.

Effective systems and processes are often the result of careful planning and design. When developing a new system or process, it's important to consider the following factors:

Objectives: What's the overall goal of the system or process? What outcomes or results are you trying to achieve?

Scope: What tasks or activities will be included in the system or process? What will be excluded?

Stakeholders: Who will be affected by the system or process? What are their needs and expectations?

Resources: What resources (e.g., people, equipment, or technology) will be required to implement the system or process?

Timing: What is the timeline for implementing and completing the system or process?

Once a system or process has been designed, it's important to implement it consistently and monitor its performance to ensure it's meeting the desired outcomes. This may involve conducting regular reviews, gathering feedback from stakeholders, and making adjustments as needed.

Effective systems and processes are essential for the smooth and efficient operation of any organisation. By providing a clear structure and framework for completing tasks, systems and operations become much easier to accomplish.

If you want your charity to run like a well-oiled machine, then you need to implement some systems and processes. In this chapter, we'll discuss the importance of creating policies and procedures, setting up financial systems, and developing human resources policies. We'll also provide advice on how to create efficient systems so you can focus on your mission.

James Clear, the author of *Atomic Habits*, said, "You do not rise to the level of your goals. You fall to the level of your systems." And this is so true when it comes to running a successful charity.

Five key systems and processes are essential to the success of any charity. Let's go over the importance of each in a bit more detail.

Policies and Procedures

Imagine if you had no system to guide the operations of your charity. How would volunteers or staff know what to do? That's why it's so important you establish policies and procedures for your organisation.
So how do you go about creating policies and procedures?

First, you'll need to identify potential areas where policies and procedures will be needed. This could include operations, finance, human resources, information technology, and so on. Then you'll want to create a document outlining the rules for each area. Make sure your document is comprehensive but also easy to read and understand.

Some best practices for policy and procedure creation include making sure you have a clear purpose for each policy, setting measurable goals, soliciting feedback from stakeholders, ensuring the policies are regularly reviewed and updated, and implementing good communication of the policies.

Financial Systems

That a successful charity requires a sound financial system cannot be overemphasised. This includes creating an organisational budget and setting up an accounting system. When setting up your budget, be sure to include all income sources, expenses, and fundraising goals.

In addition, you'll want to set up an accounting system to ensure the organisation is financially responsible. Make sure you have effective systems in place for tracking donations, grants, investments, and other income sources. You should also develop policies around how funds will be used and tracked internally.

We'll discuss this in detail later in the book.

Renowned investor Warren Buffett said, "It takes twenty years to build a reputation and five minutes to ruin it. If you think about that, you'll do things differently." The key is to have a system that all the people managing the finances in your charity are comfortable with. Set up a process for financial decisions and ensure you have the necessary controls in place to prevent fraud or abuse.

Do your due diligence when it comes to financial systems. Make sure you understand the rules and regulations of the country where you operate and make sure everything is in compliance with any applicable laws. Talk to an accountant or other financial advisor if you're unsure about anything. Most donors will need you to properly account for the money they donate to your charity, which only a good system can generate for you.

Human Resources Policies

Every charity needs policies related to hiring, managing, and developing staff. These policies should clearly outline the expectations of the organisation and provide guidance on how to handle personnel issues. As most charities implement projects with a start and end, it's essential to know how and when to employ and when to let go of staff in line with the jurisdiction and labour laws of the country you operate.

In addition, make sure you abide by all applicable employment laws when hiring and managing staff. This includes establishing minimum wage requirements, providing benefits as appropriate, adhering to anti-discrimination laws, and following any other relevant regulations. Most enthusiastic charity owners often forget to budget for the cost of delivering aid. Core to this are staff and competent personnel.

The modern workforce is constantly changing. Divergent thinking, agility, and creative problem-solving are in high demand. Make sure your human resources policies reflect the times. Establish employee development programs to provide ongoing training and create an environment that encourages collaboration and innovation.

A coherent workplace culture is also important for any charity. This includes promoting a safe and healthy work environment, providing feedback to staff members, recognising excellence, and helping employees grow in their roles. A robust human resources policy will help ensure your charity has the best possible employees to maximise its chances of success.

Information Technology Systems

In today's digital world, it's essential you have efficient information technology systems in place. You should also develop an effective system for storing and sharing data within your organisation, such as a cloud-based storage system or an internal database system. Additionally, consider investing in software solutions that can help streamline day-to-day operations, such as email systems and customer relationship management tools. This includes having secure networks to protect confidential data and protecting against cyber-attacks.

Not just the tool, the digital infrastructure also supports the foundation of your charity. Make sure you have an effective system to store and share data and information between all stakeholders, from donors to employees. Some of the best software currently on the market for managing charities include NationBuilder, Benevity, and Donorbox.

Look for the following traits when deciding on a software or management system:

- *Flexibility:* An intuitive design that can be customised to fit the needs of your organisation.
- *Security*: Strong security features to keep confidential data safe and secure.
- *Scalability*: The ability to grow with your charity as it grows in size.
- *Integrations*: Seamless integration between other third-party tools, such as accounting software or donation platforms.
- *Efficiency*: Automated processes and features to save time and money.

Developing Standard Operating Procedures

Another important aspect of running a successful charity is having standard operating procedures (SOPs) in place. These should clearly outline how different processes are handled within the organisation, such as fundraising campaigns or volunteer management.

Creating SOPs isn't difficult but it does take time and effort. Start by outlining what needs to be done for each step in a given process then document it in a clear and concise manner that everyone can easily understand. Be sure to include who has responsibility for each task and when they need it to be completed.

In addition, make sure the SOPs are regularly updated so they remain relevant and effective.

Let's look at a sample of SOPs for volunteer management:

- *Recruiting volunteers:* Outlining how to attract and recruit new volunteers.
- *Onboarding volunteers:* Providing information on training, orientation, and other onboarding activities.
- *Assigning tasks and responsibilities:* Assigning roles and tasks for each volunteer, based on their skills and preferences.
- *Monitoring progress and performance:* Setting up a system to track the progress of each volunteer and give feedback when needed.
- *Rewarding volunteers:* Establishing clear criteria for rewarding exceptional work or long service.

Similarly, something for fundraising campaigns would look like this:

- *Establishing campaign objectives:* Outlining the goals and desired outcomes of a fundraising campaign.
- *Identifying target audience:* Determining who to target with each campaign to maximise results.
- *Planning activities:* Decide on the types of activities that will be used to promote the campaign.
- *Developing materials and content:* Creating promotional materials, such as media kits, emails, or flyers.

- *Measuring success:* Assessing how effective each activity was in achieving its objectives.

By putting in place sound systems and processes, you can ensure your charity is running smoothly and efficiently. This will help you focus on your mission and reach your goals more quickly. Now let's move on to discuss developing an effective strategy for achieving success with your charity.

Systems and Processes on How to Start a Charity and Make It Work: Your First Few Steps to Impacting Lives

Setting up a charity is no small feat. It requires the cooperation of multiple individuals and organisations, as well as much time and effort. But it's also one of the most rewarding initiatives you can undertake—after all, your goal is to make an impact on people's lives, and that's something that can be incredibly fulfilling. To help you get started on your journey, let's take a look at some systems and processes for setting up a charity and making it work. From choosing which cause to support to establishing partnerships with other organisations, we'll cover the essential steps so your charity can start making a difference in people's lives.

Defining Your Success

When starting a charity, it's important to have systems and processes in place to ensure its success. Here are a few tips on how to get started:

1. *Define your mission and goals:* What do you hope to achieve with your charity? What problem are you trying to solve? Be as specific as possible so you can create targeted programs and initiatives that will help you reach your goals.
2. *Research the needs of your target population*: Who will you be helping with your charity? What are their specific needs? What programs or services can you offer that will meet those needs?
3. *Create a budget and fundraising plan:* How much money do you need to get started? How will you generate funds to support your programs and initiatives? Make sure to include a mix of different revenue streams so you're not reliant on any one source of funding.

4. *Put together a team of dedicated volunteers:* A charity is only as strong as the people behind it. Gather passionate individuals who share your vision for change and are willing to put in the hard work required to make a difference.
5. *Plan for the long term:* Don't try to do too much too soon—focus on sustainability from the start. Consider how you'll continue to operate once initial funding sources run out or when key personnel move on to other projects. Having systems and processes in place from the beginning will help ensure your charity's longevity.

Understanding the Scope of What You Want to Achieve

The first step in starting a charity is understanding the scope of what you want to achieve. What are your goals? What populations do you want to serve? What types of services do you want to provide? Once you have a clear understanding of your goals, you can begin to develop a plan for achieving them and determining how to measure success.

Your goals should be SMART. That means that you should be able to answer questions like how many people you want to help, what types of assistance you want to provide, and when you want to achieve your goals. Keep in mind, your goals may change as your charity grows and develops, so it's important to review and revise them on a regular basis.

Once you've developed your goals, you need to determine how you'll achieve them. What are the specific steps you'll take? Who'll be responsible for each task? What resources will you need? How much money will you need to raise? Answering these questions will help you develop a detailed plan for moving forward with your charity.

Putting Together a Board of Directors

Charity is not a one-man show. You need a board of directors to help you with the big decisions and day-to-day operations of your charity. But how do you put together a board of directors?
Here are a few tips:

1. *Define the role of your board:* What will they be responsible for? What kind of advice and guidance will they give? Be clear about your expectations from the start.

2. *Find individuals with the right skill set:* When choosing your board members, look for people with complementary skill sets. You want a team that can cover all the bases, from fundraising to legal issues to marketing.
3. *Consider diversity:* A diverse board brings different perspectives and experiences to the table, which can only benefit your charity. Think about race, gender, religion, and other factors when assembling your team.
4. *Give everyone a say:* Once you have your board assembled, it's important to make sure everyone feels heard. Encourage open communication and debate on the important issues facing your charity.
5. *Set guidelines for decision-making*: Establishing ground rules for how decisions will be made will help keep everyone on the same page and prevent disagreements down the road.

The Initial Stages of Building Your Team

When starting a charity, one of the most important steps you can take is building a strong team. This team will help you achieve your goals and make a lasting impact.

There are a few things to keep in mind when building your team:

1. *Make sure you have a clear vision for your charity.* This will help you attract like-minded individuals who are passionate about your cause.
2. *Find people with complementary skills.* To be successful, you'll need a diverse team with different skills and strengths.
3. *Don't be afraid to delegate tasks.* As the leader of your charity, it's important to delegate tasks and allow others to take on responsibility. This will help build a stronger team overall.
4. *Communicate regularly and openly with your team members.* This will help ensure everyone is on the same page and working towards common goals.
5. *Be willing to compromise and listen to feedback.* No team is perfect but by being open to feedback and willing to compromise, you can build a strong foundation for success.

How to Get People to Donate and Support Your Cause

When you're first starting a charity, it can be difficult to get people to donate and support your cause. However, there are a few things you can do to increase your chances of success.

First, make sure you have a clear and concise message about what your charity does and why it's important. People are more likely to donate if they understand how their money will be used and why it's needed.

Second, reach out to your personal network of family and friends and ask them to spread the word about your charity. The more people who know about it, the more likely someone is to make a donation.

Finally, don't be afraid to ask for help from others who are more experienced in fundraising. There are many resources available that can teach you how to effectively solicit donations. With some effort and planning, you can successfully convince people to donate and support your charity.

As a nonprofit organisation, fundraising is a crucial aspect of your work. It allows you to continue providing valuable services and resources to those in need and make a positive impact in your community. However, getting people to donate and support your cause can be a challenging task, especially with the abundance of organisations vying for support. Here are some tips on how to effectively get people to donate and support your cause:

Clearly articulate your mission and impact: People are more likely to donate if they understand the purpose and impact of your organisation. Make sure to clearly communicate your mission and the difference your organisation is making in the world. Highlight specific examples of how your work is making a positive impact and how donations will help further your mission.

Make a personal connection: People are more likely to donate if they feel a personal connection to your cause. This can be achieved through storytelling, which allows donors to see the human side of your organisation. Share stories of individuals who have been directly affected by your work and how their lives have been changed for the better. This can help donors feel more connected to your cause and more motivated to support it.

Offer a variety of donation options: People may have different preferences for how they would like to donate. Some may prefer to make a one-time donation, whereas others may prefer to set up a recurring donation. By offering a variety of options, you can make it easier for people to donate in a way that works best for them.

Show appreciation: Donors want to know their contributions are making a difference and that they're valued. Make sure to regularly thank donors for their support and keep them updated on how their donations are being used. This can include sending personalised thank you notes, updating them on the impact their donations are making, and inviting them to events or volunteer opportunities.

Engage with your audience: Social media and email newsletters can be great tools for staying in touch with your audience and engaging with them on a regular basis. Use these platforms to share updates, success stories, and the ways people can get involved with your organisation. This can help build relationships with potential donors and keep your cause top-of-mind.

Host events and fundraisers: In-person events and fundraisers can be a great way to raise awareness and funds for your cause. Hosting events can help people feel more connected to your organisation and provide an opportunity for them to learn more about your work. Consider hosting events such as charity runs, bake sales, or silent auctions to raise funds and engage with your community.

Partner with other organisations: Partnering with other organisations can help raise awareness and support for your cause. Look for organisations that share similar values and missions, and consider partnering on events or campaigns. This can help expand your reach and draw in new donors.

Offer incentives: Offering incentives can be a great way to encourage donations. This can include offering exclusive merchandise or experiences in exchange for donations. Consider offering tiered incentives where higher levels of donations come with more valuable perks.

Use storytelling: As mentioned earlier, storytelling can be a powerful tool for getting people to donate and support your cause. Share stories about the individuals or communities you're serving, as well as how your organisation is making a difference in their lives. This can help donors feel a personal connection to your cause and be more motivated to support it.

Appeal to emotions: People are more likely to donate if they feel emotionally invested in your cause. This can be achieved through compelling storytelling and highlighting the human side of your work. Show how your organisation is making a positive impact on people's lives and how donations can help make a difference.

Maintaining Momentum in Your Charity Work

Maintaining momentum in your charity work can be difficult but it's important to keep your eye on the prize and remember why you're doing this work in the first place. Maintaining momentum in charity work can be a challenge, especially when it comes to keeping up with the demand for services and resources. It requires dedication, perseverance, and a strong sense of purpose to continue pushing forward, even when the going gets tough. Here are some tips for maintaining momentum in your charity work:

1. *Set realistic goals for yourself and your team.* It's important to have something to strive for, but if your goals are too lofty, it can be discouraging when you don't meet them.
2. *Celebrate your successes, no matter how small they may seem.* Acknowledging even the smallest wins can help keep you motivated to continue your good work.
3. *Stay organised and efficient in your work.* This will help you make the most of your time and resources and ultimately have a greater impact on your charity work.
4. *Keep an open mind and be willing to adapt as needed.* Things will inevitably change over time, so it's important to be flexible to continue having a positive impact.
5. *Be persistent and never give up on your goals.* It's easy to get discouraged but if you believe in what you're doing, that perseverance will pay off in the end.

Starting a charity is an admirable goal and can have a profound impact on people's lives. With the right knowledge, systems, and processes in place, anyone can start their own charity and make it work. Our guide has shown you the first few steps to take when starting your journey towards positively impacting others through charitable works. If you're looking for more information or guidance on how to build out your existing project, we would be happy to help. Good luck making an impact with your charity!

In conclusion, setting up good systems and processes is essential for successful charities. Implementing policies, creating financial systems, establishing human resources policies, developing information technology systems, and creating SOPs will all help ensure your organisation runs as smoothly as possible. With these tools in place, you'll be well-equipped to focus on your mission and achieve success.

Key Takeaways

- *It's important to establish clear policies and procedures for your charity.*
- *Set up a strong financial system that includes an organisational budget, proper tracking of income sources, and effective internal controls.*
- *Develop human resources policies that comply with all applicable employment laws and promote a healthy workplace culture.*
- *Invest in digital infrastructure and software to help you manage your charity more efficiently.*
- *Create SOPs for all processes within your organisation, such as volunteer management or fundraising campaigns.*
- *Be sure to review your systems and processes regularly to ensure they're still working effectively.*
- *By taking the time to create efficient systems and processes, you can focus on doing what you do best—helping people in need through your charitable work.*
- *A system is a set of interconnected components that work together to achieve a specific goal or objective.*
- *A process is a series of steps or tasks that are followed to complete a specific task or achieve a particular result.*
- *Systems and processes are often used in businesses and organisations to improve efficiency, reduce waste, and increase productivity.*
- *When designing a system or process, it's important to consider the inputs, outputs, and desired outcomes, as well as the resources and constraints involved.*
- *It's also important to continuously monitor and evaluate the performance of systems and processes to identify and address any issues or bottlenecks.*
- *There are various tools and techniques that can be used to improve systems and processes, such as process mapping, Six Sigma, and Lean.*
- *Effective systems and processes are essential for the smooth operation of any organisation or business.*

Chapter 6
Budgeting and Financials

If you're going to start a charity, then you're going to need to know how to handle your finances. And the best way to do that is by creating a budget. A budget will help you track your income and expenses, so you can make informed decisions about how best to allocate your resources.

In this chapter, we'll cover the basics of budgeting, including how to track income and expenses, forecast future income and expenses, and create an effective budget. We'll also provide tips on budgeting best practices.

Budgeting is the process of creating a plan for managing your money. It involves setting financial goals, tracking your spending, and making adjustments to stay on track. A budget can help you save money, pay off debt, and reach financial independence.

There are several key elements to consider when creating a budget:

Income: This includes all sources of money you receive, such as your salary, investment income, and any other sources of income.

Expenses: These are the things you spend money on, such as rent, groceries, utilities, and entertainment.

Savings: It's important to set aside money for emergencies, retirement, and other long-term goals.

Debt: If you have any outstanding debts, such as credit card balances or student loans, it's important to include these in your budget.

To create a budget, start by tracking your spending for a few weeks to get a sense of where your money is going. This can be done using a spreadsheet, budgeting app, or even pen and paper. Once you have a clear understanding of your income and expenses, you can start making adjustments to your spending habits to reach your financial goals.

There are several different methods for budgeting, including the 50/30/20 rule, which suggests allocating fifty per cent of your income to necessities (such as rent and bills), thirty per cent to discretionary spending (such as dining out and entertainment), and twenty per cent to savings and debt repayment.

Another approach is the envelope system, where you allocate a certain amount of cash to envelopes labelled for different expenses (such as groceries, gas, and entertainment) and only spend the money in those envelopes. This can help prevent overspending and encourage mindful spending.

It's also important to regularly review and update your budget to ensure it's realistic and achievable. This may involve adjusting your spending habits, finding ways to increase your income, or setting new financial goals.

Managing your finances can be challenging but with a solid budget and a little discipline, it's possible to achieve financial stability and reach your financial goals. So always try to be mindful of your spending and saving habits and seek out resources and advice to help you make informed financial decisions.

Have you ever felt like you're always trying to make ends meet? Are your bills piling up faster than you can afford to pay them? Do you feel like there's never enough money? It can be tough staying afloat in a sea of debt but that doesn't mean it's impossible. With the right budgeting and financial planning, you can stay on top of your bills and get back on track. Let's go over some of the basics of budgeting and financials so you can take control of your finances and make sure your money is working for you.

What are Some Budgeting Tips for Charities?

Budgeting is one of the most important aspects of running a charity. Here are some tips to help you stay on track:

1. *Know your income and expenses.* This seems like a no-brainer but it's important to keep track of both your income and expenses. This will help you know where your money is going and where you can cut back, if necessary.
2. *Have a realistic budget.* Don't try to stretch your resources too thin by overspending in one area and underspending in another. Make sure your budget is realistic and achievable.

3. *Prioritise your spending.* Not all expenses are created equal. Make sure you're prioritising the area's most important to your mission.
4. *Keep fundraising in mind.* Fundraising should be a regular part of your budgeting process, not an afterthought. Make sure you have allocated enough resources to this critical activity.
5. *Stay flexible.* Things change, both internally and externally, so it's important to stay flexible with your budgeting plans. Be prepared to make adjustments as needed so you can continue to operate effectively.

How to Make Your Charity Sustainable

It costs money to run a charity, and that money needs to come from somewhere. To ensure your charity is sustainable, you need to ensure it has a reliable source of income. There are a few ways to do this:

1. *Diversify your funding sources.* Don't rely on just one or two donors. Try to get support from a variety of individuals, businesses, foundations, and government grants.
2. *Create a budget and stick to it.* Know how much money you need to operate each year and plan where that money will come from. Make sure you have a cushion in case unexpected expenses come up.
3. *Keep your overhead low.* The less you have to spend on things like rent, utilities, and staff salaries, the more money you'll have to put towards your mission.
4. *Raise awareness of your charity.* The more people know about your organisation, the more likely they are to support it financially. Use social media, PR campaigns, and events to get the word out there.
5. *Be transparent with your finances.* Donors want to know where their money is going and how it's being used. Be open about your budget and expenditures so they can see their donation is making a difference.

The Difference Between a Nonprofit and a For-Profit Business

There are a few key differences between nonprofits and for-profit businesses. For starters, nonprofits don't have shareholders like for-profits do. This means the primary focus of a nonprofit is not to make money for its owners but rather to further its mission. Additionally, nonprofits are exempt from paying many taxes that for-profit businesses have to pay. This is because the government recognises nonprofits provide a public good or service. Finally, nonprofits must disclose their financial information to the public, whereas for-profit businesses don't have to.

Budgeting and financial literacy are essential skills for anyone to have, regardless of age or income level. Creating a budget is the first step towards taking control of your finances and increasing your financial security in the long run. By mapping out exactly where your money goes each month, you can find ways to reduce spending and save more money while still achieving all your financial goals. With budgeting tools like *Mint*, it's easier than ever to get started with creating a budget and taking control of your finances.

A nonprofit organization serves a specific social cause or group of individuals instead of generating profit. Often referred to as charities, nonprofit organizations depend on donations, gifts, and grants to finance their operations, necessitating the establishment of budgets and targets. In contrast, for-profit businesses are set up with the primary goal of generating income for owners or shareholders. For-profit businesses typically generate revenue by selling goods or services to customers and they're required to pay taxes on any profits they earn.

There are several key differences between nonprofits and for-profit businesses:

Purpose: As mentioned above, the main difference between nonprofits and for-profit businesses is their purpose. Nonprofit organisations are set up to serve a specific social cause or group of individuals, whereas for-profit businesses are set up to generate income for their owners or shareholders.

Funding: Nonprofit organisations rely on donations and grants to fund their operations, whereas for-profit businesses generate revenue by selling goods or services to customers.

Structure: Nonprofit organisations are typically structured as either a 501(c)(3) organisation or a public charity. These types of organisations are exempt from paying federal income tax and are required to follow specific rules and regulations set forth by the IRS. For-profit businesses, in contrast, can be structured as a sole proprietorship, partnership, corporation, or limited liability company, and they're required to pay taxes on any profits they earn.

Decision-making: Nonprofit organisations are typically governed by a board of directors, who make decisions on behalf of the organisation. For-profit businesses, in contrast, are typically owned and operated by one or more individuals, who have complete control over the direction and decision-making of the business.

Profits: Nonprofit organisations are not allowed to distribute profits to their directors, officers, or members. Any surplus funds generated by a nonprofit organisation must be used to further the organisation's mission and achieve its charitable objectives. For-profit businesses, in contrast, can generate profits and distribute them to their owners or shareholders as dividends.

Public perception: Nonprofit organisations are often viewed as being more altruistic and community-minded than for-profit businesses because they're not motivated by profit and are instead focused on serving a specific social cause. For-profit businesses, in contrast, are perceived as being more focused on maximising profits and are often less trusted by the public.

Transparency: Nonprofit organisations are required to disclose their financial information and activities to the public because they rely on donations and grants to fund their operations. For-profit businesses, in contrast, are not required to disclose their financial information to the public unless they're publicly traded companies.

Oversight: Nonprofit organisations are subject to oversight by state and federal regulatory agencies, including the IRS, which ensures they're meeting their charitable objectives and following all relevant laws and regulations. For-profit businesses are subject to oversight by various regulatory agencies, depending on the type of business and the industries in which they operate.

In conclusion, nonprofit and for-profit businesses are fundamentally different in terms of their purpose, funding, structure, decision-making, profits, public perception, transparency, and oversight. Nonprofit organisations are set up to serve a specific social cause or group of individuals, whereas for-profit businesses are set up to generate income for their owners or shareholders. Nonprofit organisations rely on donations and grants to fund their operations, whereas for-profit would self-fund, borrow from friends, apply for loans from banks or approach the stock exchange to fund their operations.

What is Budgeting?

Budgeting is the process of allocating your financial resources to achieve your financial goals. It involves setting a budget and sticking to it to stay on track.

A budget is a plan that tells you how you'll spend your money. It's important to set a budget so you can track your progress and ensure you're staying on track with your financial goals.

There are many different ways to budget but the most important thing is to find one that works for you and stick to it. You may need to experiment with different methods before you find one that fits your lifestyle and helps you reach your financial goals.

The Benefits of Budgeting

Budgeting is one of the most important aspects of financial planning. A budget can help you track your spending, stick to a savings plan, and make smarter choices about your money.

There are many benefits to budgeting, including the following:

- *Knowing where your money is going:* A budget can help you track your spending and see exactly where your money is going. This can be helpful in identifying areas where you may be able to cut back or save more money.
- *Staying on track with your savings goals:* A budget can help you stay disciplined with your savings goals. By tracking your spending and setting aside money each month for savings, you can make progress towards your financial goals.
- *Making better decisions about your money:* Budgeting can help you make more informed choices about how to spend and save your money. When you have a clear picture of where your money is going, it can be easier to make choices that align with your financial goals.

How to Create a Budget

Assuming you don't have a budget:

1. You should determine your income. This is everything you make in a month from your job, tips, child support, spousal support, investments, and so on.
2. Next, you need to make a list of your expenses. Include both fixed expenses (mortgage/rent, car payment, insurance) and variable expenses (food, gas, entertainment).
3. Following this, you should subtract your total monthly expenses from your total monthly income. If the number is positive, you have extra money to work with each month. If the number is negative, you need to find ways to cut back on your spending or increase your income.
4. Once you know how much money you have to work with each month, start allocating it towards different categories: savings, retirement, debt payoff, and so on. Don't forget to include a buffer for unexpected expenses!

Tracking Your Progress

When it comes to your finances, it's important to keep track of your progress so you can stay on track and make necessary adjustments. Here are a few ways to do this:

- *Review your budget regularly.* This will help you see where you're spending your money and where you can cut back.
- *Set up a system to track your income and expenses.* This can be as simple as using a spreadsheet or an app like Excel, Mint, or YNAB.
- *Check-in with yourself periodically to see how you're doing.* Are you sticking to your budget? Are you saving enough money? Are there any areas where you need to make changes?

Tips for Sticking to Your Budgets

When it comes to budgeting, there are a few key things to keep in mind to stay on track. First and foremost, be realistic with your budget. It's important to set a budget you can actually stick to, rather than one that's overly restrictive and difficult to maintain.

Another important tip is to track your spending. This will help you see where your money is going and identify any areas where you may be able to cut back. There are a number of ways to do this, including using a budgeting app or simply tracking your expenditures in a notebook.

It can also be helpful to have a specific savings goal in mind. When you know what you're saving for, it can be easier to resist the temptation to spend unnecessarily. Finally, remember budgeting is a process and it may take some time to get the hang of it. Be patient with yourself and stick with it—over time, it'll become second nature to you!

Budgeting and financials are an important part of our lives that we often take for granted. Learning how to budget your money wisely, save carefully, and invest strategically can help you reach all your goals in life. Whether it's achieving financial freedom, retiring early, or just having enough money to go on vacation once a year, getting the basics of budgeting and finance down will put you well on your way to success. So why not get started today?

Make a budget: The first step to sticking to your budget is creating one. Start by listing all your monthly income sources and fixed expenses, such as rent, bills, and debt payments. Then, factor in your variable expenses, such as groceries, entertainment, and transportation costs. Don't forget to include savings in your budget as well.

Track your spending: Once you have a budget in place, it's important to track your spending to ensure you're staying on track. This can be as simple as keeping a written record of your expenses or using a budgeting app to automatically track your spending.

Cut unnecessary expenses: Look for ways to trim your budget by cutting out unnecessary expenses. For example, you might be able to save money by cancelling subscriptions or memberships you no longer use or by switching to a cheaper cell phone plan.

Find ways to save on fixed expenses: Although it's not always possible to reduce fixed expenses like rent or mortgage payments, there may be ways to save on these costs. For example, you might be able to negotiate a lower rate on your rent or refinance your mortgage to get a lower interest rate.

Look for discounts and deals: Don't be afraid to negotiate or shop around for the best prices on goods and services. You might be able to save money by using coupons, taking advantage of sales, or negotiating lower prices on products or services.

Set financial goals: Setting financial goals can help you stay motivated to stick to your budget. Whether you're saving for a down payment on a house, paying off debt, or building up your emergency fund, having a specific goal in mind can help you stay focused on your budget.

Find ways to increase your income: If you're struggling to stick to your budget, consider finding ways to increase your income. This could mean taking on additional work, starting a side hustle, or asking for a raise at your current job.

Enlist the help of a financial advisor: If you're having trouble sticking to your budget, consider seeking the help of a financial advisor. A financial advisor can help you create a budget that works for your specific financial situation and offer advice on how to reach your financial goals.

Get support from friends and family: It can be tough to stick to a budget on your own, especially if you're used to a certain lifestyle. Consider enlisting the support of friends and family to help you stay on track. They can offer encouragement, accountability, and even ideas for how to save money.

Stay positive and stay committed: Sticking to a budget can be challenging but it's important to stay positive and stay committed. Remember the effort you put into budgeting now will pay off in the long run.

Distinguish Nonprofit Budgeting from For-Profit Budgeting

There's a slight difference between nonprofit and for-profit budgeting. Whereas for-profit companies focus on the bottom line, nonprofits tend to be focused more on mission and impact. Nonprofits should use budgets that are able to support their long-term objectives and track both income and expenses to measure their progress towards those goals.

Nonprofit budgeting is the process of creating a financial plan for a nonprofit organisation that outlines its income and expenses to achieve its goals and objectives. Nonprofit budgeting typically focuses on the allocation of resources to various programs and initiatives that align with the organisation's mission and values.

For-profit budgeting, in contrast, is the process of creating a financial plan for a for-profit organisation that outlines its income and expenses to generate profits. For-profit budgeting typically focuses on maximising profits by optimising the allocation of resources to various business activities that generate revenue. It is very normal in for-profit projects to start with a business case and a very well-elaborated business plan.

There are several key differences between nonprofit and for-profit budgeting:

- *Purpose*: Nonprofit budgeting is focused on achieving the organisation's mission and goals, whereas for-profit budgeting is focused on maximising profits.
- *Funding*: Nonprofit organisations rely on donations and grants to fund their programs and initiatives, whereas for-profit organisations generate revenue through the sale of goods or services.
- *Expenses*: Nonprofit organisations typically allocate a higher percentage of their budgets to program expenses, whereas for-profit organisations allocate a higher percentage of their budgets to operating expenses.
- *Return on Investment*: Nonprofit organisations don't seek to generate a return on investment, whereas for-profit organisations aim to generate a positive return on investment for shareholders.
- *Governance*: Nonprofit organisations are typically governed by a board of directors, whereas for-profit organisations are typically governed by a board of directors and shareholders.

The accountability that comes with budgeting for nonprofit organisations is different from that of for-profit companies. Instead of focusing on profits and shareholder value, nonprofits should be thinking about how their actions will affect the mission they set out to achieve in the first place. So how do we go about creating a budget?

Break Down Your Budget Components

The first step in creating a budget is to break down your budget components into categories, such as expenses and income. This will help you identify and track any potential areas of waste or inefficiency.

In a typical budget, we'll have three main components: operating expenses, capital expenditures, and administrative costs. Operating expenses are those the charity needs to operate on a day-to-day basis, such as salaries and office rent. Capital expenditures are projects or investments that require larger amounts of money upfront, such as purchasing new equipment or building renovations. Administrative costs cover any overhead related to running the organisation, like accounting software, insurance premiums, and legal fees.

Once you have broken down your budget components into categories, it's time to start breaking them down by programs and departments. This will help you keep track of where the money is going and identify any areas that may need additional funds or more efficient allocation of resources.

There are many different components that can make up a budget, but some common ones include the following:

Income: This includes all sources of money you receive, such as salary, wages, tips, investments, and any other forms of income.

Expenses: This includes all the money you spend, including bills, rent or mortgage payments, food, transportation, and entertainment.

Savings: This is the amount of money you set aside for long-term goals, such as retirement or a down payment on a home.

Debt payments: This includes any money you need to pay off loans or credit card balances.

Taxes: This includes any taxes you need to pay, such as federal, state, and local taxes.

Insurance: This includes any insurance premiums you need to pay, such as health insurance, car insurance, or home insurance.

Charitable donations: This is any money you choose to give to charitable organisations or causes.

Miscellaneous: This category includes any other expenses that don't fit into the other categories, such as gifts or personal grooming.

Fixed Budget Reviews

Fixed budget reviews refer to the process of reviewing a project or budget that has a predetermined, fixed amount of funds allocated to it. This means the project or budget cannot exceed the allocated amount, and any additional funds must be approved through a separate process.

The purpose of a fixed budget review is to ensure the project stays within the allocated funds and that all resources are being used efficiently. It also helps identify any potential cost overruns or issues that may arise during the project.

The review process typically involves reviewing the project plan, budget, and any relevant financial documents. The team or individual responsible for the project may also be asked to provide updates on progress and any challenges that have arisen.

Fixed budget reviews are important for a number of reasons. They help keep projects on track and ensure they're completed within the allocated funds. They also help identify any potential issues or challenges that may arise, allowing for corrective action to be taken before they become major problems. Finally, they help ensure the project is being managed efficiently and effectively, which can help improve the overall quality of the final product or service.

Your budget should be reviewed and updated on a regular basis, at least on a monthly or quarterly basis. This will help you identify any areas where funds are being allocated inefficiently or new projects need funding. Fixed budget reviews also allow you to ensure all expenses are accounted for and tracked properly.

Although these are the fundamentals of creating a budget for your nonprofit organisation, there are other ways to ensure your financial decisions support your mission.

The Seven Principles of Effective Budgeting

The following seven principles can help you create a budget that's sustainable and supports your long-term objectives.

Deciding on the Approach

This includes considering any external constraints and developing an understanding of the resources available to you. You may opt for a top-down approach, which involves starting with a global view and then working down into more detailed subsections, as needed. Or if you're working with limited resources or are just getting started, you may opt for a bottom-up approach, which involves starting small and building up from there. Consistency is essential in this process because budgeting for your nonprofit should be done on a regular basis.

There are a few factors to consider when deciding on the approach to take when tackling a problem or task:

- *Time:* How much time do you have to devote to this task? If you have a tight deadline, you may need to choose a quicker approach.
- *Resources*: What resources do you have at your disposal? Do you have a team of people to help, or are you working alone? Do you have access to all the tools and materials you need?

- *Scope*: How large is the problem or task? If it's a big project, you may need to break it down into smaller, more manageable chunks and take a phased approach.
- *Prioritisation*: What's the priority of this task? If it's urgent or critical, you may need to prioritise it over other tasks and allocate more resources to it.
- *Feasibility*: Is the approach you're considering realistically achievable? Consider any potential challenges or obstacles that may arise and whether you have the skills and expertise to overcome them.
- *Flexibility*: Can you be flexible in your approach if things don't go as planned? Is there room for iteration and adjustment as you work on the task?
- *Effectiveness*: Will the approach you're considering be the most effective way to solve the problem or complete the task? Consider any potential benefits or drawbacks of different approaches and choose the one that will provide the best results.

Evidence-Based Budgeting

Evidence-based budgeting is a budgeting process that relies on data and research to inform financial decisions. It's designed to ensure public resources are being used in the most effective and efficient manner possible.

Evidence-based budgeting involves gathering data and information to inform your financial decisions. This could include data on the effectiveness of different programs, the expected return on investments, or any other relevant metrics that can help you make more informed decisions. A good example of this is gathering data from surveys or focus groups to find out which programs are most effective for achieving your mission.

To implement evidence-based budgeting, policymakers and budget analysts gather data and research on the costs and outcomes of different programs and policies. They then use this information to identify the most effective and cost-efficient options and allocate resources accordingly.

One key aspect of evidence-based budgeting is the use of performance measures to track progress and assess the impact of different programs. This allows policymakers to make informed decisions about which programs are working well and which may need to be adjusted or eliminated.

Some benefits of evidence-based budgeting include the following:

Improved resource allocation: By using data and research to inform financial decisions, policymakers can ensure resources are being directed towards the programs most likely to achieve their intended outcomes.

Increased transparency and accountability: Evidence-based budgeting requires policymakers to be open and transparent about their budgeting decisions—and to justify those decisions based on evidence. This can help increase public trust and accountability.

Greater efficiency: By focusing on the most effective and cost-efficient programs, evidence-based budgeting can help governments achieve better outcomes while also reducing costs.

Overall, evidence-based budgeting is a promising approach to financial decision-making that can help governments achieve better results and better serve the needs of their citizens.

Take the following example: If you want to measure the effectiveness of a new youth outreach program, you may need to collect data on how many young people participated in the program and discover what impact it had on their lives. This information can then be used to inform future budgeting decisions.

Diversification of Income Sources

Diversification of income sources refers to having multiple sources of income rather than relying on just one. This can provide financial stability and protection against economic downturns or unexpected circumstances that may impact one income stream.

Having a diversified income can come in the form of having multiple streams of employment, starting a side business, investing in real estate or stocks, or renting out a property. Diversification can also involve balancing different types of income, such as passive income, which requires little ongoing effort, and active income, which requires ongoing effort.

Having diversified income sources can provide financial security and allow individuals to pursue their passions and interests while still maintaining a stable financial foundation. It can also allow for greater flexibility and freedom in terms of career and lifestyle choices.

It's important to diversify your income sources to reduce the risk of relying too heavily on one source. When creating a budget, consider the different ways you can generate income, such as donations, grants, sponsorships, and fundraisers. This will help ensure your nonprofit has several streams of revenue and is not overly reliant on any single source.

At least three major sources of income are recommended for a successful budget. These can range from donations to grants to sponsorships and even to fundraisers.

Automating Expenses

Automating expenses is a great way to save time and money. By automating recurring expenses, you can reduce the amount of manual tracking and free up resources for other tasks. This could include anything from setting up automatic payments for rent or purchasing software subscriptions on a monthly basis.

Direct transfers reduce the friction associated with collecting money and can be a great way to ensure all your payments are made on time. Automating expenses can save time and reduce the risk of errors. Here are some ways to automate expenses:

- *Set up automatic payments for recurring bills*: This includes utility bills, rent, and other expenses that are the same amount each month.
- *Use a budgeting app or software*: These tools can track your expenses and alert you when bills are due. Some even allow you to pay bills directly through the app.
- *Use a credit card for all expenses*: This can simplify tracking expenses because all charges will appear on a single statement. Just be sure to pay off the balance each month to avoid interest charges.
- *Use online banking to pay bills*: Many banks offer online bill pay, which allows you to schedule payments in advance and view all your bills in one place.
- *Set up automatic transfers to savings*: By setting up automatic transfers to a savings account, you can save money without having to remember to transfer funds manually.

Automating expenses can help you stay organised, reduce the risk of missed payments, and free up time for other tasks. Just be sure to regularly review your automated expenses to ensure everything is accurate and up-to-date.

Risk Management

The fifth principle is risk management. This involves identifying the potential risks that can impact the success of your organisation and developing strategies for how to mitigate them. Risk management includes anything from making sure contracts are up-to-date and properly executed to having contingency plans in place in case of a financial emergency.

Risk management is the process of identifying, assessing, and prioritising potential risks to minimise or eliminate their impact on an organisation or project. This involves identifying the potential risks that may arise, evaluating the likelihood and impact of these risks, and developing strategies to mitigate or eliminate them.

There are several key steps involved in risk management:

- *Identifying risks:* This involves identifying all the potential risks that may arise in a project or organisation. This can be done through brainstorming sessions, reviewing past experiences, or using risk assessment tools.
- *Assessing risks*: Once the risks have been identified, they need to be assessed in terms of their likelihood and impact. This helps with prioritising the risks and determining which ones need to be addressed first.
- *Prioritising risks:* After assessing the risks, they need to be prioritised based on their likelihood and impact. This helps determine which risks need to be addressed first and which resources should be allocated to them.
- *Developing risk mitigation strategies*: Once the risks have been prioritised, strategies need to be developed to mitigate or eliminate them. This can involve creating contingency plans, implementing controls or procedures, or purchasing insurance.
- *Monitoring and reviewing risks*: Ongoing monitoring and review of risks is necessary to ensure they're being effectively managed. This includes monitoring the effectiveness of risk mitigation strategies, reviewing the risk profile of the organisation or project, and adjusting strategies, as needed.

We'll go over the details of risk management within the context of charities in the later sections of the book.

Flexibility for Adjustments

Flexibility for adjustments is the ability to adapt and make changes, as needed, to achieve a desired outcome or goal. This can be especially important in situations where there may be unexpected challenges or changes in the environment.

For example, if a company is planning to launch a new product but there are unexpected delays in production, it may need to be flexible in adjusting its marketing and sales strategies to ensure they still meets its target launch date. If one of your programs starts gaining traction and you receive more funds than originally anticipated, you'll need to create a plan for how those additional funds will be allocated. This could include expanding the program or investing in new initiatives.

Having flexibility for adjustments can also be helpful in personal situations, such as when one's plans for the day are disrupted by unforeseen circumstances. In these cases, being able to adjust and come up with alternative plans can help minimise stress and ensure goals are still achieved.

Rigid budgets can be difficult to sustain and may not account for unexpected changes in the external environment. It's important to remember no budgets are set in stone and they should be easy to adjust based on changing circumstances.

Overall, flexibility for adjustments is an important skill to have to adapt to changing circumstances and achieve success.

Robust Financial Management System

A robust financial management system is a system able to handle a wide range of financial transactions and operations, including budgeting, forecasting, accounting, and reporting. It should be able to handle large amounts of data and complex financial calculations with ease and be able to produce accurate and reliable financial reports on demand.

Some key features of a robust financial management system include the following:

- *Advanced budgeting and forecasting capabilities:* The system should be able to handle complex budgeting and forecasting scenarios, including the ability to create multiple scenarios and compare them side by side.
- *Comprehensive accounting capabilities*: The system should be able to handle all major accounting tasks, including accounts payable, accounts receivable, general ledger, and payroll.
- *Advanced reporting capabilities*: The system should be able to produce a wide range of financial reports, including balance sheets, income statements, cash flow statements, and more.
- *Customisation options*: The system should allow users to customise financial reports and dashboards to meet their specific needs and requirements.
- *Integration with other systems*: The system should be able to seamlessly integrate with other systems and software, such as CRM, HR, and project management systems.

The final principle is to ensure you have robust financial management systems in place. This includes having protocols for recording and tracking income and expenses, clearly defined roles and responsibilities within the organisation, and effective internal controls.

Developing a financial system can seem overwhelming at first but there are many resources available to help you get started. These include software solutions such as QuickBooks or accounting firms that specialise in nonprofit finance. Overall, having a robust financial management system is an essential tool for any business looking to streamline its financial operations and make more informed financial decisions.

Tracking Income and Expenses

Tracking income and expenses is an important aspect of managing your finances. It helps you understand where your money is coming from and where it's going, so you can make informed decisions about your financial future.

To track your income and expenses, you can use a variety of methods. One option is to use a budgeting app or software, which can help you keep track of your spending and income automatically. Alternatively, you can use a spreadsheet or a notebook to manually record your income and expenses.

To get started, you'll need to gather all of your financial records, including bank statements, bills, and receipts. Then, you'll need to categorise your income and expenses into categories, such as rent, groceries, transportation, and entertainment.

Once you have all your information organised, you can start tracking your income and expenses. This can help you identify areas where you may be overspending or areas where you can save money.

It's also a good idea to regularly review your income and expenses to ensure you're on track with your financial goals. This may involve setting up budgets, creating financial plans, or working with a financial advisor to help you reach your financial goals.

Overall, tracking your income and expenses can be a valuable tool for managing your finances and achieving your financial goals. By understanding where your money is coming from and where it's going, you can make more informed decisions about your financial future and take control of your financial well-being.

When it comes to tracking your income and expenses, there's no one-size-fits-all approach. Every charity's needs are unique, so you'll need to design a system that works best for you. The most important thing is to have some way of accumulating information on both sides—income *and* expenses.

One option is to use accounting software such as QuickBooks or FreshBooks. These programs allow you to easily track your incoming revenues and outgoing costs in an organised manner. This can be especially helpful if you plan on claiming tax deductions for donations received by the organisation.

Another option is to use Excel spreadsheets or Google Sheets. This requires more manual input from you since the data must be entered into the spreadsheet manually, but it's still a useful option for tracking income and expenses.

Finally, you could also use a combination of paper and electronic records. For example, you may want to keep receipts in physical form (e.g., in an envelope or shoebox) while also entering the data into a digital platform like QuickBooks.

Whichever method you choose, make sure to document everything so you can access it with ease when needed. This will help ensure all your financials are up-to-date and accurate at all times.

Forecasting Future Income and Expenses

When budgeting, it's important to consider both your current financial status and your future financial status. This means taking the time to forecast your expected income and expenses over a period of time.

When forecasting future income, you should consider both existing and potential sources of revenue. For existing sources, look at past performance to get an idea of what might happen in the future. For potential sources, think about the ways you might be able to bring in more money (e.g., launching a new fundraising campaign).

When forecasting expenses, consider both fixed costs (e.g., rent or payroll) and variable costs (e.g., supplies or advertising). This will help you better plan for the future and ensure you have enough resources available when needed.

Forecasting future income and expenses can be a useful tool for managing your personal or business finances. It involves making estimates about the amount of money you expect to receive (income) and pay out (expenses) in the future. This can help you make financial decisions, set goals, and plan for the future.

To forecast your future income and expenses, you can start by reviewing your current financial situation. Look at your income sources, such as your salary, investments, and other sources of income. Consider any changes that might affect your income in the future, such as a promotion, raise, or change in your employment status.

Next, consider your expenses. Make a list of all your recurring expenses, such as rent or mortgage payments, utilities, insurance, and other bills. Look for ways to reduce your expenses by cutting costs or finding more affordable options.

Once you have a good understanding of your current financial situation, you can begin to make estimates about your future income and expenses. You might want to create a budget or financial plan to help you track your progress and make adjustments, as needed.

Keep in mind that forecasting is not an exact science and your future income and expenses may not turn out exactly as you expect. It's important to be realistic and flexible and be prepared for unexpected changes or events that could affect your financial situation. The key to successful budgeting is having accurate information at all times. With the right tools and strategies, you can ensure your charity always stays in the black.

Key Takeaways

- *Separating your budget components into categories, such as expenses and income, will help you identify and track any potential areas of waste or inefficiency.*
- *It's important to diversify your income sources to reduce the risk of relying too heavily on one source.*
- *Automating expenses can save time and money.*
- *Direct transfers are a great way to ensure payments are made on time.*
- *Risk management involves identifying the potential risks that could affect the success of your organisation and developing strategies to mitigate them.*
- *The budget should be flexible enough to adjust based on changing circumstances.*
- *Forecasting future income and expenses will help you plan for the long-term success of your organisation.*
- *Start by setting financial goals for yourself. This will help you stay motivated and focused on what you want to achieve with your money.*
- *Create a budget that works for you. This means figuring out how much money you have coming in and going out each month and adjusting your spending accordingly.*
- *Keep track of your expenses. This will help you see where you're spending the most money and where you might be able to cut back.*
- *Avoid overspending by making a list of what you need before you go shopping and sticking to it.*
- *Save for the future. It's important to set aside money for emergencies and for long-term goals like retirement.*
- *Pay off any high-interest debt as soon as possible. This will help you save money in the long run and improve your financial stability.*
- *Don't be afraid to ask for help. If you're struggling with budgeting or financial planning, there are resources available to help you get back on track.*
- *Plan for the unexpected. Life can be unpredictable, so it's important to have a plan in place for unexpected expenses or emergencies.*
- *Educate yourself about personal finance. There are many resources available to help you learn more about budgeting, saving, and investing.*

- *Keep your budget up-to-date. Your financial situation is likely to change over time, so make sure you're keeping your budget current to reflect those changes.*

Chapter 7
Fundraising

Fundraising is the process of collecting funds or money from various sources to support a specific cause, organisation, or project. This can be done through a variety of methods such as charitable donations, fundraising events, crowdfunding campaigns, or selling products or services. Fundraising is often used to support nonprofit organisations, schools, or other charitable causes, but it can also be used for personal or business purposes. The goal of fundraising is to generate sufficient funds to support the intended cause or project.

If there's one thing all charities need, it's money. Although there are a number of ways to raise money, fundraising is by far the most important. That's because fundraising allows charities to do what they do best: help others.

In 2022, the worldwide funds raised by charities exceeded $2 trillion. That figure is staggering and it shows just how powerful fundraising can be.

When it comes to fundraising, there are a few different methods you can use. The most common include grant writing, crowdfunding, special events, and capital campaigns. Each of these has its own benefits and drawbacks, so here's an overview of each one.

But before that, the most important thing is to have a streamlined and efficient process in place to capture potential donors and solicitation. The best charities in the world all have a well-defined donor journey, from initial contact to donation. Knowing your donors and engaging them in meaningful conversations is key.

Grant Writing

Perhaps the most popular means of fundraising in the handbook, grant writing is an effective way to secure funding for your charity. Grants are typically offered by foundations, government agencies, bi-lateral and multi-lateral institutions, and other organisations, and they can be a great source of income for charities.

Grant writing is the process of writing a proposal for funding from a grant-making organisation, such as a government agency, foundation, or nonprofit. The purpose of grant writing is to persuade the organisation to fund your project or program by demonstrating its merit, feasibility, and alignment with the organisation's goals and values.

Grant writing involves researching potential funding sources, developing a clear and concise proposal, and creating a budget and timeline for the proposed project. It also involves writing compelling narratives and demonstrating the need for the project, as well as the potential impact and outcomes it will achieve.

Grant writers must be skilled in writing, research, and problem-solving, as well as effectively communicating the value and significance of the project. They must also be able to adhere to grant guidelines and meet deadlines.

Successful grant writing requires a thorough understanding of the grant-making organisation's mission and priorities, as well as the needs of the community or population the project will serve. It also requires careful planning and execution, as well as the ability to effectively communicate the project's value and potential impact.

The process of applying for grants involves researching potential funders, preparing applications, and submitting the required documents. It takes time, effort, and resources to apply for them correctly—but it's worth it in the end.

The best way to write a grant application is to focus on the problem your charity seeks to solve. Here's a quick sample of how to structure it:

- *Step 1:* Outline the problem your charity seeks to solve.
- *Step 2:* Describe the activities and services you'll provide to solve this problem.
- *Step 3:* Estimate the costs involved in providing these services.
- *Step 4:* Explain why you need funding from this specific funder and how the money will be used.

Crowdfunding

In recent years, crowdfunding has become an increasingly popular way for charities to raise money quickly. Sites like Kickstarter and GoFundMe allow users to collect funds from friends, family, and even strangers by setting up a campaign page online.

Social media has opened the world of crowdfunding to a much wider audience. Plus, the whole process is incredibly easy—all you need to do is create an account and start sharing your campaign. People can donate in just a few clicks, meaning you can reach thousands of potential donors in no time at all.

The only downside is that crowdfunding campaigns are often short-lived, so it's important to act fast if you want to make the most of them.

A good crowdfunding campaign should have the following elements:

- *Step 1:* Create an eye-catching and informative campaign page.
- *Step 2:* Share your campaign on social media and other online platforms.
- *Step 3:* Set clear goals for the campaign, such as a target amount of money or number of donations.
- *Step 4:* Keep donors informed of your progress and let them know how their donation is making a difference.

Storytelling is the most important aspect of a successful crowdfunding campaign. You need to be able to explain why your charity exists and what it hopes to achieve to engage potential donors. Having a unique theme for your campaign can also help it stand out from the crowd.

Special Events

Organising special events is a great way to raise awareness and funds for your charity at the same time. They can range from small, local gatherings to large-scale conferences or galas, depending on how much you're looking to raise.

Events are an excellent opportunity to attract new donors and strengthen relationships with existing ones. Plus, they give you the chance to network with other like-minded organisations and individuals who may be interested in supporting your cause.

When planning an event, there are several key elements that need to be taken into consideration:

- *Step 1:* Set clear goals for what you want to achieve.
- *Step 2:* Decide on the type of event and its scope.
- *Step 3:* Ensure you have a good budget in place to cover costs.
- *Step 4:* Promote your event using both online and offline channels.
- *Step 5:* Hire reliable professionals, such as caterers, DJs, or photographers.
- *Step 6:* Thank your sponsors and donors for their support.

Capital Campaigns

A capital campaign is a major fundraising initiative that typically covers large-scale projects like building renovations or new facilities. They are complex processes that require careful planning, professional advice, and dedicated time from all involved parties.

Capital campaigns are fundraising efforts aimed at raising a large amount of money over a specified period of time, typically several years, for a specific purpose or project. These campaigns are often used by nonprofit organisations and charities to fund major initiatives, such as building renovations, new facilities, or program expansion.

While capital campaigns can be a challenging and time-consuming undertaking, they can also be extremely rewarding and help a charity achieve its long-term goals and objectives. Here are some key considerations for planning and executing a successful capital campaign:

Define the project and the need: Before launching a capital campaign, it's important to clearly define the project or initiative the campaign will support. This includes identifying the need for the project, outlining the benefits it will provide, and determining the costs associated with it.

Set realistic goals: Determine how much money needs to be raised and over what period of time. It's important to set realistic goals that can be achieved through the campaign, rather than setting unrealistic goals that may discourage donors or lead to disappointment.

Create a campaign plan: Develop a detailed plan that outlines the steps and activities needed to achieve the campaign's goals. This should include a timeline, budget, marketing plan, and strategies for engaging donors.

Identify potential donors: Research and identify potential donors who may be interested in supporting the campaign. This includes individuals, foundations, corporations, and other organisations.

Engage and cultivate donors: Engage with potential donors through personal meetings, events, and other outreach efforts. Foster relationships with these donors and keep them informed about the campaign's progress and impact.

Launch the campaign: Once the campaign plan is in place and potential donors have been identified, it's time to launch the campaign. This may include announcing the campaign to the public, holding fundraising events, and reaching out to donors through various channels.

Monitor progress and adjust as needed: Keep track of the campaign's progress and make adjustments as needed to ensure the campaign stays on track. This may include adjusting the campaign plan, reaching out to new donors, or identifying new fundraising opportunities.

Show gratitude: Thank donors for their support and keep them informed about the impact of their contributions. This helps foster a sense of connection and keeps donors engaged in the campaign.

Maintaining a charity's financial stability can be a challenging task, and capital campaigns can be a valuable tool for raising the funds needed to support long-term initiatives and projects. By following these steps and being proactive in your fundraising efforts, you can effectively plan and execute a successful capital campaign that helps your charity achieve its goals and make a positive impact in your community.

The important part is having a clear vision of what you want to achieve and a detailed plan to make it happen. You also need to identify potential major donors who can contribute significantly towards the goal.

The capital campaigns require much more diligence and research than others. Here are the main steps involved:

- *Step 1:* Set realistic goals and a timeline for the campaign.
- *Step 2:* Hire dedicated professionals such as architects, designers, or accountants to help with different aspects of the campaign.
- *Step 3:* Analyse your current resources and develop a strategy for fundraising.
- *Step 4:* Research potential donors who might be interested in supporting your cause.

- *Step 5:* Create promotional materials such as brochures or flyers to make them aware of your project.
- *Step 6:* Present your case to major prospects and secure their commitment towards the campaign.
- *Step 7:* Follow up regularly with all stakeholders throughout the process.

Major Grants

Major grants or gifts are large donations given to charitable organisations for the purpose of supporting their work and mission. These gifts can be given by individuals, businesses, or foundations and they often play a critical role in helping charities achieve their goals and make a positive impact on their communities.

There are many different ways major gifts can be used by charities, including funding new programs and initiatives, supporting ongoing operations, and providing financial assistance to those in need. Some charities may use major gifts to finance specific projects, such as building a new facility or expanding their services, whereas others may use these donations to support their general operations and cover the day-to-day expenses.

Regardless of how major gifts are used, they're essential for helping charities achieve their goals and make a lasting difference in the lives of those they serve. At this point, let's explore some of the key ways major gifts (this can also be referred to as grants) can be used to maintain charities and ensure their ongoing success.

Fundraising efforts: Major gifts can be a crucial source of funding for charities and they can be used to support a variety of fundraising efforts. These efforts may include traditional methods such as events and campaigns, as well as newer techniques like crowdfunding and online fundraising. Major gifts/grants can help charities meet their fundraising goals and provide the resources they need to continue their work.

New programs and initiatives: Major gifts can be used to fund new programs and initiatives that help charities expand their reach and impact. For example, a major gift might be used to launch a new service or program that helps meet the needs of specific communities or populations. By providing the resources needed to implement these programs, major gifts can help charities make a difference in the lives of many people.

Ongoing operations: Major gifts can also be used to support the ongoing operations of charities, covering the costs of day-to-day expenses such as rent, utilities, and staff salaries. These gifts can help charities maintain their current levels of service and ensure they're able to continue to make a positive impact in their communities.

Special projects: Many charities have special projects they're working on, such as building new facilities or expanding their services. Major gifts can be used to fund these projects and help charities achieve their goals. By providing the necessary resources, major gifts can help charities make a lasting impact in their communities.

Emergency funding: Charities may sometimes encounter unexpected expenses or emergencies that require additional funding to address. Major gifts can help provide the resources needed to handle these situations and ensure charities are able to continue their work, without interruption.

Capacity building: Major gifts can also be used to help charities build their capacity and improve their operations. This may include funding training and professional development for staff, investing in new technologies or equipment, or supporting strategic planning efforts. By building capacity, charities can become more effective and efficient in their work, which can ultimately lead to greater impact.

In addition to these specific uses, major gifts can also help charities build relationships with donors and other supporters, which can be valuable for their long-term success. Donors who make major gifts may be more likely to continue supporting a charity in the future and they may also be more likely to spread the word about the organisation to their own networks.

Overall, major gifts play a vital role in helping charities achieve their goals and make a positive impact on their communities. By providing the resources needed to fund new initiatives, support ongoing operations, and address emergencies and special projects, major gifts can help charities maintain their work and ensure their ongoing success.

Harvard professor and fundraising expert, Robert Solomons, once said, "Major gifts represent the lifeblood of many organisations." This is especially true for charities which rely heavily on donations from wealthy individuals or corporations.

Naming major gifts after the donor or offering them a seat on the charity board are great ways to show your appreciation for their support. It also helps build long-lasting relationships with potential donors and encourages them to continue giving in the future.

To secure major gifts you need to do the following:

- *Step 1:* Develop a profile of your ideal major donor.
- *Step 2:* Research potential prospects who match this profile.
- *Step 3:* Ask around in your network and establish connections with these prospects.
- *Step 4:* Make sure all communication is personalised and sincere.
- *Step 5:* Schedule one-on-one meetings with each contact to discuss your project in more detail.
- *Step 6:* Follow up with each donor and thank them for their support.
- *Step 7:* Identify ways to build a long-term relationship with the donor.

No matter which fundraising method you choose, it's always important to create a unique and engaging experience for your donors. After all, if you want to stand out from the crowd, you need to give people something special they can't find anywhere else.

The Donor Journey

The entire above is just a means to an end; the ultimate goal of fundraising is to make a connection with potential donors and entice them to support your cause. They're only effective if you can effectively bring donors along in their journey towards giving.

The lifetime value of a donor is far greater than the initial donation they make, so it's important to think of them as partners in your cause. Donor stewardship is key—keep donors informed of your progress and show appreciation for their support.

The best-learned practices to ensure a successful donor journey start before the first contact. You have to have a clear vision for the future of your cause and be able to clearly communicate it. You also need to create a personalised experience for each donor that's tailored to their needs and interests.

Let's walk over a prospective donor who works in venture capital and has expressed an interest in supporting your charity. The first step is to reach out and schedule a meeting. Make sure you provide ample information about your organisation and the work it does so they can make an informed decision.

When meeting with potential donors, be prepared to answer questions they may have and address their concerns. You should also anticipate any objections they may bring up, such as cost or time commitments, and have good responses ready at hand.

Be sure to thank them for their time after the meeting. A follow-up email or phone call goes a long way!

From there, keep in touch with regular updates on how the money is being used and remind them of the impact their support has had on your cause. For every new event or project, invite them to join or share it with their network. Make sure to thank them for any donation they make and celebrate any milestone successes you achieve together.

Throughout the process, maintain a genuine appreciation for your donors—this will go a long way in building relationships and encouraging future support from them.

Fundraising is an essential part of running a charity. With the right amount of dedication and creativity, you can create engaging campaigns that excite potential donors and help generate funds for your cause. Whether it's writing grants, organising crowdfunding campaigns, or engaging in major gift-giving opportunities, there are plenty of ways to raise money for your charity—it just takes some effort to find what works best!

Key Takeaways

- *Fundraising is essential for charities to exist and thrive.*
- *There are a variety of ways to raise funds, such as grant writing, crowdfunding, special events, and capital campaigns.*
- *It's important to have a streamlined process in place for identifying potential donors and soliciting donations.*
- *When it comes to crowdfunding, storytelling is key—make sure you explain the problem your charity seeks to solve and why people should donate.*
- *It's also important to give major donors a special experience, such as naming gifts after them or offering them seats on the charity's board.*
- *To be successful in fundraising, it's essential you have dedicated personnel and resources to ensure the process runs smoothly.*
- *Being organised and having an optimistic attitude will also go a long way towards achieving your goals.*

- *Start early: Planning and preparing for a fundraising campaign can take time, so it's important to start as early as possible. This will give you more time to research potential donors, craft a compelling pitch, and establish relationships with potential supporters.*
- *Research your audience: Understanding your audience and their interests is key to successful fundraising. Identify potential donors and tailor your pitch to their interests and values.*
- *Set clear goals: Before beginning your fundraising campaign, be sure to set clear and specific goals. This will help you stay focused and ensure you're working towards a specific purpose.*
- *Create a budget: Having a budget in place will help you manage your resources and track your progress. Be sure to account for all expenses, including marketing, event costs, and staff time.*
- *Utilise social media: Social media platforms can be a powerful tool for fundraising. Use them to spread the word about your campaign, share updates and stories, and engage with potential donors.*
- *Use storytelling: Telling a compelling and emotional story can help engage potential donors and make your campaign more memorable. Use real-life examples and statistics to illustrate the impact of your work.*
- *Foster relationships: Building relationships with potential donors is key to successful fundraising. Take the time to get to know them and their interests, and make an effort to stay in touch and update them on the progress of your work.*
- *Follow-up: Don't be afraid to follow up with potential donors. A polite and personalised follow-up can often be the key to securing a donation.*
- *Show appreciation: Showing appreciation to donors is important to build trust and maintain relationships. Thank them for their support and provide updates on how their contribution is making a difference.*
- *Keep track of your progress: Keep track of your progress and be sure to celebrate your successes along the way. This will help keep you motivated and focused on your fundraising goals.*

Chapter 8
Marketing and Communications

If there's one thing all charities need after fundraising, it's a good marketing and communications strategy. Unfortunately, many charities don't realise the importance of marketing until it's too late. By then, they've already missed out on valuable opportunities to reach their target audience. A properly executed marketing and communications plan can help your charity reach its goals and gain credibility.

Good marketing and communications hinges on six key points: developing a brand, creating marketing materials, using social media, developing a marketing plan, brand messaging, and media relations. Cohesion between all of these elements is essential to make sure your message resonates with the right audience.

Developing a Brand

Credibility is the biggest element of any brand, and this is especially true for charities. A strong, unified brand helps portray your charity as professional, trustworthy, and organised. Branding can also be used to differentiate you from other organisations within the same sector. Your branding should clearly reflect the goals of your organisation and inspire people to take action or donate.

A good charity always has five major things that depict its brand or identity—credibility, uniformity, goals, consistency, and dedication. Although these elements may be intangible qualities that may not always be seen at first glance, they're what make a charity stand out from the rest.

So how does one build a brand? The following four points can help you get started:

1. *Research your competition, the market, and potential donors.*
2. *Determine what makes your charity unique.*
3. *Develop a visual identity for your charity that reflects its purpose and goals.*
4. *Implement these elements across all your marketing materials to create a cohesive brand image.*

Next, a good brand has a loyal following and the trust of its audience. The larger the following, the more exposure and recognition your charity will have. To gain this trust and following, you must create a memorable brand message that resonates with people's emotions.

Creating Marketing Materials

Marketing materials refer to any item that helps promote your charity or organisation. Common materials include printed brochures, flyers, postcards, and even digital assets such as videos, banners, or images for use on websites and social media platforms. These can all be used to stimulate interest in your cause by highlighting the key features of why someone should donate or volunteer for your charity.

Creating marketing materials involves several steps:

Identifying your target audience: It's important to know who your marketing materials will be directed at. This will help you tailor your message and design to appeal to your specific audience.

Defining your brand: Your marketing materials should reflect your brand's values, mission, and personality. Make sure you have a clear understanding of your brand before you start creating marketing materials.

Developing a message: Determine what you want to say to your audience and how you want to say it. Be clear and concise and make sure your message resonates with your target audience.

Designing your materials: Choose a design that fits your brand and message. This can include choosing colours, fonts, images, and layout.

Printing and distributing your materials: Once you have finished designing your marketing materials, it's time to print and distribute them. This can include printing flyers, brochures, business cards, and other materials, as well as distributing them through email, social media, or in-person events.

Evaluating the effectiveness of your materials: After you've distributed your marketing materials, it's important to evaluate how well they worked. This can include tracking website traffic, sales, and other metrics to see if your materials were successful in reaching and engaging your target audience.

When creating these marketing materials, it's important to keep two things in mind—consistency and clarity. Your branding should be consistent across all of your materials so everything looks unified and professional. In addition, your message should be clear and concise so people understand your mission quickly and are driven to act on it.

Using Social Media

In today's digital age, social media is one of the most important and effective tools for getting the word out about your charity. With a well-crafted message on the platforms your target audience is using, you can reach thousands of people in a matter of minutes. Not only does it allow you to spread awareness about your cause and engage directly with potential supporters but also allows you to build relationships with other charities and influencers who can help amplify your message.

Now a lot of charities want to get everything right the first time but creating a successful social media presence is something that takes time and practice. It's important to be patient and consistent in your messaging, listen to your audience, and respond quickly to their feedback. Also, be sure you focus on quality over quantity—one great post can get more attention than a dozen mediocre ones!

To get the best results, the digital media strategy should have most of the following elements:

Trifecta of targeting: Target your message to the right people at the right time in the right way. This involves understanding who's most likely to be interested in supporting your charity and then delivering relevant content that resonates with them. It also means timing it correctly, knowing what platforms they're using, and engaging with them on a consistent basis.

Engagement: It's not just about getting followers; it's about having meaningful conversations with them and engaging with their feedback. Make sure to reply quickly so they know you're listening. Ask questions, create polls, initiate contests or other activities—anything that encourages engagement will help build relationships with your audience.

Content strategy: Focus on creating content that isn't just promotional but can actually help people learn more about your cause. Try to come up with creative ways to show how your charity is making an impact in the world or provide helpful advice and resources related to your mission.

Analytics: Track key metrics such as clicks, views, impressions, shares, and followers so you can know what's working and what isn't. Knowing which of your posts are successful will help you create better content in the future, as well as inform decisions about where to focus your efforts for maximum impact.

Platform-specific strategies: Every social media platform is different, so make sure you tailor your message for each one. For example, Twitter is great for sharing quick updates and engaging with the community, whereas Instagram is visual-heavy and works well for showcasing stories in pictures or videos.

With some careful planning and creative messaging, you can use social media to spread awareness of your cause to a wider audience—as long as you remember it's not just about quantity but quality too. Have fun with it and don't be afraid to experiment!

Developing a Brand Messaging

Your brand messaging is the way in which you communicate who you are and what makes your charity unique. It should give potential supporters a sense of why they should care about what you do and why they should support your cause.

Uniqueness is key—you want to be able to stand out from the other charities in your space. Think about what makes your charity unique and how best to communicate that message. Is it the impact of your work or the values you stand by? Brainstorm different ideas and think about which ones resonate with you most strongly.

Once you've identified your brand messaging, make sure it's consistent across all your communication channels—website, social media posts, press releases, and so on. This will help create a unified look and feel for your charity that will help people recognise who you are at a glance. Finally, take some time to review and refine your messaging periodically so it continues to stay fresh and relevant to what's happening in the world.

- *Define your target audience:* Who's your brand trying to reach? Consider demographics, interests, and pain points.
- *Identify your brand values*: What are the core beliefs and values that drive your brand? These should be reflected in all of your messaging.
- *Develop a brand personality*: How do you want your brand to be perceived by your target audience? This can include tone, style, and overall vibe.
- *Determine your brand messaging*: What message do you want to convey to your target audience? This should be clear, consistent, and unique to your brand.
- *Create a messaging hierarchy*: Prioritise the key messages you want to convey and consider how to effectively communicate them through various channels.
- *Test and iterate*: Test your messaging with small groups and gather feedback. Use this feedback to refine and improve your messaging strategy.
- *Integrate your messaging across all channels*: Ensure your messaging is consistent across all touchpoints, including your website, social media, advertising, and customer interactions.

Media Relations

The media can be a powerful ally in helping you spread awareness of your cause and increase engagement with members of the public. Being featured in news outlets, magazines, or other publications can give your charity a major boost because it will reach an audience that may not have been aware of you otherwise.

To get the attention of the press, start by researching which media outlets would be most interested in covering your story. This means looking at their existing content to get an idea of what topics they cover and building relationships with journalists who write about similar issues. You should also create compelling stories that highlight the impact and importance of your work—writing inspiring profiles, compelling news articles, or thought-provoking opinion pieces will help you stand out from the competition.

Creating a media plan is also important because it will help you stay organised and focused on achieving your goals. Think about how long you'll be trying to get press coverage, what type of stories you want to tell, which journalists and publications you'll be targeting, and when and how often you will reach out—these are all things that need to be considered for your media relations strategy to be successful.

Key Takeaways

- *Marketing and communications are essential for any charity to spread awareness of its cause and engage with members of the public.*
- *Developing a strong brand, creating marketing materials, using social media strategically, developing a marketing plan and engaging in media relations are all key elements of successful marketing and communications.*
- *Make sure you track key metrics to know what's working and what isn't, tailor your message for each platform, create compelling stories that highlight the impact of your work, and develop a media plan to stay organised.*
- *With some careful planning, creative messaging and persistence, you can effectively promote your charity to the public!*

Chapter 9
Team Building

Team building is an important aspect of any organisation because it helps create a cohesive and productive team that can work effectively towards achieving common goals. It involves the process of creating a positive work environment that fosters collaboration, communication, and trust among team members. This process is essential for the success of any team because it helps improve morale, increase productivity, and reduce conflicts within the team.

There are several ways to build a strong and effective team, including creating a shared vision, setting clear goals and expectations, providing support and resources, and promoting collaboration and communication.

One of the first steps in team building is creating a shared vision for the team. This involves defining the team's purpose and goals and ensuring all team members understand and buy into this vision. This shared vision should be communicated clearly and consistently to all team members and should be used to guide the team's actions and decisions.

Setting clear goals and expectations is another important aspect of team building. It's important to establish specific and measurable goals for the team and communicate these goals to all team members. This helps ensure everyone is working towards the same objectives and there's no confusion about what needs to be achieved. It's also important to establish clear roles and responsibilities for each team member and provide support and resources to help them meet their goals.

Providing support and resources is essential for building a strong and effective team. This includes providing training and development opportunities, as well as access to the tools and resources team members need to do their jobs effectively. It's also important to provide ongoing support and feedback to team members to help them grow and develop in their roles.

Promoting collaboration and communication is another key aspect of team building. This involves creating an open and inclusive work environment where team members feel comfortable sharing ideas and working together towards common goals. This can be achieved through regular team meetings, open communication channels, and opportunities for team members to collaborate on projects and tasks.

In addition to these strategies, several other activities can help build a strong and effective team. These include teambuilding exercises, such as outdoor activities and team sports, which can help build trust and foster teamwork. Team retreats and off-site meetings can also be effective in helping team members get to know each other better and build stronger relationships.

Effective team building also involves managing conflicts within the team. This may involve addressing conflicts directly and finding ways to resolve them, as well as promoting a positive and respectful work culture that promotes teamwork and collaboration.

Overall, team building is a critical aspect of any organisation and is essential for the success of any team. By creating a shared vision, setting clear goals and expectations, providing support and resources, and promoting collaboration and communication, organisations can build a strong and effective team that can work together effectively towards achieving common goals.

If you want to start a charity, it's important to build a great team to support you. A team of talented and dedicated individuals can help you achieve your mission and make a real difference in the world. But assembling such a team can be tricky—it takes time, effort, and careful planning. In this chapter, we'll discuss how to go about building the perfect team for your charity. We'll cover everything from managing staff to training and development. So read on and learn how to put together the ultimate dream team!

The Psychology of Teams

Before we dive into the details, let's take a moment to consider team dynamics. Building an effective team requires understanding how teams work, as well as the psychology behind them. A successful team has to have a clear goal or mission—something all members can rally around. It also needs leadership, trust between members, and open communication so everyone can stay on track. Without these essential elements, your team won't reach its full potential.

A key ingredient in the modern workforce is having people with divergent skillsets working together. Diversity is essential for creativity, problem-solving, and making sure everyone contributes their fair share. So when building your team, make sure you include people with different backgrounds and experiences—it can work wonders!

The next most important factor is the diversity of culture—it's important to respect and celebrate differences and make sure everyone feels included. With the right mix of people, your team will be set up for success.

Managing Staff

Once your team is in place, it's important to manage them properly. This means setting clear expectations and goals—everyone should know what's expected of them and how their work contributes to the wider picture. It also involves providing guidance and support, where necessary, and celebrating successes when they come.

Productivity expert and author Charles Duhigg suggests creating a 'cadence' of regular check-ins and feedback loops (11). This encourages open communication and allows everyone to stay on the same page. Research backs up this approach, showing regular check-ins can reduce turnover by up to thirty-five per cent.

Make sure you have an organisational chart that outlines the roles and responsibilities of each staff member so everyone knows who to go to with questions or concerns. You may also want to consider developing a performance review system so you can track progress over time and make sure everyone is meeting their targets.

Fixed pay-for-performance and other compensation strategies can also help ensure everyone is on the same page when it comes to success. Establishing clear metrics for each role and offering performance bonuses can help motivate employees and improve productivity.

Creating an environment where everyone feels supported and valued is essential when building and managing a strong team. With the right tools at your disposal, you can have a team that's motivated, loyal, and well-equipped to help bring your charity's mission to life.

Building a Board of Directors

Building a board of directors is a crucial step in the development of any organisation. A board of directors is a group of individuals who are responsible for providing strategic direction, oversight, and guidance to the organisation. The board is also responsible for ensuring the organisation is financially sound and is meeting its goals and objectives.

There are several key factors to consider when building a board of directors. These include the size of the board, the skills and expertise of the members, and the diversity of the board.

Size of the Board

The size of the board of directors will depend on the size and complexity of the organisation. For small organisations, a board of three to five members may be sufficient. For larger organisations, a board of seven to nine members may be more appropriate. It's important to ensure the board is not too large because this can lead to difficulties in decision-making and communication.

Skills and Expertise

The skills and expertise of the board members are also important to consider when building a board of directors. The board should have a diverse range of skills and expertise that reflect the needs of the organisation. This may include expertise in financial management, legal issues, marketing, or human resources. It's also important to have board members with diverse backgrounds and perspectives to ensure all perspectives are considered when making decisions.

Diversity

Diversity is also important when building a board of directors. This includes diversity in terms of gender, ethnicity, age, and other factors. A diverse board can bring a wide range of perspectives and experiences to the table, which can be beneficial for the organisation.

In addition to these factors, there are several steps organisations can take to build a strong board of directors:

Define the Role of the Board

It's important to clearly define the role of the board of directors and to communicate this to potential board members.

This includes outlining the responsibilities of the board, as well as the expectations for attendance and participation in meetings.

Identify Potential Board Members

Once the role of the board has been defined, organisations can begin identifying potential board members. This can be done through networking, word of mouth, or by using a recruiting firm. It's important to identify individuals who have the skills and expertise the organisation needs, as well as commitment to the mission and values of the organisation.

Evaluate and Select Board Members

Once potential board members have been identified, organisations should conduct a thorough evaluation process to ensure they're the right fit for the organisation. This may involve conducting interviews, checking references, and reviewing resumes. It's important to select board members who are committed to the mission and values of the organisation and who are willing to make a long-term commitment.

Onboard New Board Members

Once board members have been selected, it's important to onboard them effectively. This may involve providing them with training and resources to help them understand their roles and responsibilities, as well as the policies and procedures of the organisation. It's also important to ensure board members have the support they need to be successful in their roles.

Review and Evaluate the Board

Finally, it's important to periodically review and evaluate the board of directors to ensure its functioning effectively. This may involve conducting surveys or evaluations of board members to gather feedback, as well as conducting regular performance reviews. By regularly reviewing and evaluating the board, organisations can identify any areas for improvement and take steps to address any issues.

In conclusion, building a board of directors is an important step in the development of any organisation. Start by considering factors such as the size of the board you need, and the skills and expertise of board members because you'll need a board of directors to provide guidance and oversight. A good board will bring expertise in financial management, legal affairs, fundraising, marketing, and other key areas. It's important to find individuals who can commit long-term—ideally for at least two or three years—so your charity has the stability it needs to succeed.

You could follow by putting together a list of potential candidates from your social networks: friends, colleagues, or past employers who may be interested in serving on your board. Then invite them for an interview and find out what they can bring to the table. Tell them how you intend to engage them in the oversight, how many times they may need to meet and the details of their role and responsibilities.

Once you've decided on the members of your board, it's important to ensure everyone is following the same mission. Make sure all new directors are aware of the charity's purpose and values, and that everyone has a shared understanding of where it should be heading.

The purpose of a board of directors isn't to do the legwork themselves—it's to provide advice, guidance, and oversight. Make sure you have a system in place for managing the board, such as regular meetings or online communication channels. This will help keep everyone informed and ensure your charity is on track with its vision.

Training and Development

A team is only as good as the skills its members possess, so it's important to ensure your staff is up-to-date and proficient in their roles. Training can take the form of formal instruction or mentoring, depending on the complexity of the skill you want them to learn. Providing employees with opportunities for growth and development shows you're invested in their success, which in turn increases morale and loyalty.

When it comes to team training, getting everyone on the same page is key. Make sure to provide a clear outline of objectives and expectations before diving into a session so everyone knows what they need to accomplish. Designing activities tailored to each individual's learning style helps keep things engaging.

One particular skill that can be beneficial to focus on is communication. Strong communication between team members makes collaboration easier and helps foster a positive work atmosphere. This could be something as simple as making sure everyone has the chance to speak up in meetings or it could be more advanced, like teaching everyone active listening skills.

Team training can provide a significant boost to any charity's success, so don't forget to put some thought into how your staff grows and develops. With well-rounded employees who possess the right skills, your organisation will have all the tools it needs to reach its goals.

Team Dynamics

Hierarchies seem like a thing of the past but to have a successful charity it's important to have clear roles and teams. It's not enough just to have people on board, they need to be able to work together and support each other.

One thing to note here is that team dynamics don't just happen, they need to be created. Having a team that's aligned with the goals of your charity is vital and will help you achieve your mission quickly and effectively.

One way to create a healthy team dynamic is to ensure everyone knows their role so there are no misunderstandings or conflicting ideas. It's also important everyone feels part of the team and understands how their individual contribution fits into the bigger picture. This can be achieved by ensuring each person has clear objectives, and that these objectives are regularly discussed and reviewed throughout the year, if necessary.

The social element of a team is as important as the individual roles. Make sure regular team meetings are conducted and that everyone gets a chance to speak up and offer their opinion on matters. Trust, openness, and effective communication between team members are also key to creating a successful team dynamic.

Conflict Resolution

Team building is all about finding the right mix of talents and personalities to ensure your charity stays on track and achieves its goals. But what happens when those same personalities clash? It's inevitable but managing these conflicts is an important aspect of running a successful team. Conflict resolution is key to preventing disputes from derailing progress or creating a toxic work environment.

The benefits of good conflict resolution are evident—it helps maintain morale, prevent misunderstandings, foster collaboration and understanding, and reduce stress levels in the workplace. It's also worth noting that unresolved conflicts can lead to tension or even animosity between staff members, which is something you want to avoid at all costs.

When dealing with disputes among team members, the following framework proposed by the Harvard Business Review can be useful:

1. *Seek to understand what's going on*: Ask questions, take time to listen, and explore the underlying causes of the dispute.
2. *Address miscommunications*: Misunderstandings are often the root of many conflicts, so it's important to ensure everyone is speaking a common language and understanding each other.
3. *Identify any shared interests*: There may be underlying common goals or interests that were overlooked in the heat of a disagreement. Bringing these out into the open can help bridge divides between differing opinions.
4. *Agree on how to move forward*: Once everything has been discussed and clarified, create an action plan for resolving differences and taking action.

Let's quickly run over a mock scenario of a conflict resolution process:

Let's say two of your team members, Sam and Anna, have opposing views on a certain strategy. You can start the conversation by asking them both to explain their positions and why they disagree. From there, explore any miscommunications or emotions that may be fuelling the disagreement. Is there something else you're both worried about? Is there any potential shared ground that can be built upon?

Once everything is discussed and clarified, you can come up with an action plan for resolving the differences and moving forward. Sam and Anna might decide to take a break from their debate to think it over, or they could create a new strategy that takes into account both of their points of view. However it works out, the main goal is to find a solution that everyone agrees on so you can move past the conflict and get back on track.

Conflict resolution is an important part of team building—it's essential for creating a positive environment and keeping your team focused on achieving its goals. By following the above steps, you can ensure disputes between staff members don't derail progress or create a toxic work environment. Investing the time to understand and manage conflicts will go a long way towards ensuring the success of your team.

The backbone of a successful charity is the team of people who support it, and team building is the key to creating a powerful force capable of making an impact in the world. Through effective management, and training. and development; fostering good communication and understanding between staff members; and implementing conflict resolution strategies when disputes arise, you can create a winning team that's unified around a common goal. With the right mix of talent and personalities working together, your charity will be well on its way to achieving its mission.

Key Takeaways

- *Building an effective team requires understanding how teams work, as well as the psychology behind them.*
- *Diversity of skillsets and culture is essential for creativity, problem-solving, and making sure everyone contributes their fair share.*
- *Have a performance review system in place to track progress over time.*
- *Fixed pay-for-performance strategies can help ensure everyone is on the same page when it comes to success.*
- *Creating an environment where everyone feels supported and valued is key to building a strong team.*
- *Establishing a system of trust, openness, and communication between team members is essential for team dynamics.*
- *Conflict resolution is an important part of team building—it's essential for creating a positive environment and keeping your team focused on its goals.*

Chapter 10
Volunteer Force

The social and humane element of our society makes us all human. There's no better way to express this than through volunteerism. Whether you're starting a charity or want to lend your support, volunteers can be invaluable to achieving the desired objectives.

When outreach and events are carried out, the permanent team barely makes up ten to fifteen per cent of the workforce. The other eighty-five to ninety per cent rely heavily on volunteers' dedication to the cause. Recruiting volunteers can sometimes be difficult, but if managed well, they can bring in a lot of enthusiasm and drive to help you reach your goals faster.

This chapter will discuss the importance of volunteers and how to recruit, manage, train, and recognise them for their efforts.

The Volunteer Force was a volunteer military organisation established in the United Kingdom in 1859. It was created in response to the perceived threat of invasion by France and it was intended to supplement the regular army in times of national emergency. The Volunteer Force was made up of men who were willing to serve as soldiers on a voluntary basis, and it was a popular organisation in the United Kingdom throughout the late 19th and early 20th centuries.

The Volunteer Force was established by the Militia Act of 1852, which had been passed in response to concerns about the inadequacy of the regular army in defending the country against foreign invasion. The Militia Act authorised the creation of a volunteer force of men willing to serve as soldiers on a part-time basis. The Volunteer Force was intended to be a supplement to the regular army, rather than a replacement for it, and it was intended to be used only in times of national emergency.

The Volunteer Force was made up of men who were between the ages of eighteen and forty-five, and who were willing to commit to serving as soldiers on a part-time basis. Volunteers were required to undergo a period of training, and they were expected to be available for service when needed. The Volunteer Force was organised into units that were known as corps and each corps was made up of several companies of volunteers. The corps were divided into various categories based on their location and they were given different responsibilities, depending on the needs of the local community.

The Volunteer Force was a popular organisation in the United Kingdom and it attracted many men interested in serving their country. The Volunteer Force was seen as a way for men to serve their country without having to commit to full-time military service, and it was also seen as a way for men to improve their physical fitness and learn new skills. Many men who joined the Volunteer Force were also attracted by the sense of camaraderie and the opportunity to serve with like-minded individuals.

The Volunteer Force played a significant role in the United Kingdom during the late 19th and early 20th centuries. It was used to supplement the regular army during times of national emergency, and it was also used to provide assistance during times of natural disaster. The Volunteer Force was also used to provide security during major events, such as sporting events and royal visits.

The Volunteer Force was disbanded in 1908 and it was replaced by the Territorial Force. The Territorial Force was similar to the Volunteer Force in many ways but it was intended to be a more professional organisation that was better equipped to meet the needs of the modern military. The Territorial Force was made up of men who were willing to serve as soldiers on a part-time basis and it was organised into units similar to those of the Volunteer Force.

The Volunteer Force played a significant role in the history of the United Kingdom and it's remembered as an important part of the country's military heritage. The volunteers who served in the force were highly motivated and dedicated individuals willing to serve their country on a voluntary basis, and their contributions to the defence of the United Kingdom will always be remembered.

Borrowing from this, charities and NGOs have a robust volunteer roster list composed of individuals willing to contribute time out in the field. Many are young people looking to start their trade in the humanitarian sector; others are faith-based volunteers or retired citizens who are prepared to volunteer some of their time yearly and commit some financial resources from time to time to help the people in most need. The Voluntary Service Overseas, a UK-based charity; the Nigerian Foreign Affairs funded Technical Aid Corps; and the US-government-led Peace Corps are popular among youths and professionals.

Early charities like the Red Cross movement relied heavily on mobilising volunteers, and it's also still popular among medical practitioners working on Mercy Ships and working with the Médecins Sans Frontières (Doctors Without Borders).

Recruiting Volunteers

Having a proper recruitment process in place is key to ensuring your charity's success. An effective plan includes identifying who you want to target as volunteers—focus on people with certain skillsets or unique experiences who can help boost the efficacy of your campaign. Also, consider the kind of environment you're trying to create at your charity—think about enthusiasm, commitment, and diversity.

This way, even during tough times, potential volunteers will see an opportunity to learn something new or develop their skillsets. Setting clear expectations from volunteer roles is also essential for them to understand what they can expect from the experience and what's expected of them.

A great place to start the recruitment process is by leveraging the power of social media. Use online tools to create an appealing post or video about your charity and its values that can get potential volunteers excited. Particularly helpful is highlighting the experience volunteers can gain from being involved in your charity.

Managing Volunteers

Managing volunteers is essential to reach the goals of your charity. What's the use of having thousands of people show up for a clean-up drive if they all fail to do the job?

This is where having an effective management system in place comes into play. It's important to have clear directions and tasks set out for volunteers so everyone knows what they need to do and can work together efficiently and effectively.

Creating a volunteer program with specific roles and responsibilities can be extremely useful in managing volunteers. Create action plans and assign regular tasks with deadlines to keep them motivated and on track. Of course, communication is key here—make sure to communicate clearly, provide feedback regularly, and address any questions or concerns swiftly.

Let's say you're conducting the clean-up drive, as mentioned above. Before the drive, conduct briefs to ensure everyone is on the same page and understands their roles. During the drive, have supervisors manage any issues that may arise. Following up once it's over to ask for feedback and suggestions will also help you improve your volunteer management system in future activities.

A key part of this is having the tools to manage volunteers effectively.

Training Volunteers

Training volunteers is key to having an effective and reliable volunteer force. Volunteers should not only be trained to do their job but also knowledgeable about the mission, philosophy, and goals of your charity. Having well-versed volunteers in what you're trying to accomplish will make it easier for them to help spread the message and reach your target audience.

When training volunteers, there are several important aspects to consider. You can't train volunteers on the fly—you need to create a clear plan of action that provides the necessary information and tools for them to do their job. You should also consider any special needs or requirements they might need to carry out their responsibilities effectively.

There's a key point to note here. Don't overdo it. Volunteering should be a positive experience for everyone involved, so keep the training manageable and engaging. You also want to create an environment that encourages learning by providing resources and feedback that will allow volunteers to grow and refine their skills.

Recognising Volunteer Efforts

No matter how hard you work to recruit, manage, and train volunteers, they'll be nothing but hollow shells if their efforts go unrecognised. Appreciation and recognition are the most powerful motivators for inspiring people to get involved in charitable activities.

Feeling good is a basic human need, and when volunteers feel appreciated for their efforts in supporting your charity, they'll be more likely to continue their commitment. Recognition can take many forms: from an official award ceremony to a simple thankyou note.

Award ceremonies are great opportunities to recognise the achievements of your volunteers and build relationships with them. You should also make sure you have a plan for recognising excellence in volunteering on an ongoing basis. This could include publicly thanking individuals or groups who go above and beyond what's expected or highlighting exceptional contributions on social media and other platforms.

You should also ensure any recognition you give is meaningful, appropriate, and tailored to the individual's effort as much as possible—such as congratulating volunteers who recruited new members or recognising those who have given a lot of their time to the cause.

Ultimately, volunteer recognition should be integral to your charity's culture. It will show your volunteers you value and appreciate their hard work and dedication to the cause, thus fostering loyalty between them and your organisation. With this strategic approach, you can ensure your volunteers remain an important part of the team for many years.

Motivation and Retention

Targeting the right people is essential for any volunteer force. Without passionate, motivated volunteers willing to devote their time and energy, it'll be difficult to achieve your charity's goals. However, many organisations face the challenge of recruiting and retaining volunteers over time.

To ensure you get the best possible volunteers with the right skillset and motivation, create a clear outline of what you expect from them and what they can expect in return. This helps set expectations early on so everyone is on the same page going into the arrangement.

Investing in new outreach can be costly and time-consuming, so it's important to put effort into maintaining relationships with current volunteers. Offer incentives and rewards for longer-term commitments, such as leadership roles for those who've been with the charity over a certain period of time.

Creating a volunteer program can also help keep volunteers engaged and motivated. This could include hosting regular teambuilding events or offering opportunities to get involved in different aspects of the organisation. Additionally, recognising their efforts through awards or public recognition can help ensure your volunteers feel appreciated for their hard work and dedication.

With the right strategies in place, you should be able to maintain a strong volunteer force that's passionate about your cause and will support it long into the future.

Creating an Effective Volunteer Program

Apart from what we've already discussed, designing an effective volunteer program is key to having a successful charity. Structure the program to meet your organisation's goals and objectives while ensuring volunteers can access the resources they need to carry out their tasks.

It also helps ensure there are clear guidelines for volunteers so they know exactly what's expected of them. This will help minimise misunderstandings and prevent any issues from arising down the road.

Having a volunteer management system is an effective way to manage the recruitment, training and deployment of volunteers. It can also track and monitor progress, offering you and your volunteers a reliable way to stay organised.

Finally, ensure communication between you and your volunteers is open and transparent. This will help foster better relationships and enable you to quickly address any problems or concerns they may have.

Ultimately, having an effective volunteer program in place is essential for running a successful charity. By following these tips, you can ensure your organisation has the resources it needs to recruit and retain passionate volunteers willing to support your cause for many years to come.

Key Takeaways

- *Volunteers are essential for the success of any charity.*
- *It's important to have a well-planned recruitment process to attract and retain volunteers.*
- *Volunteers need to be managed, trained, and recognised to motivate them to stay with your charity.*
- *Creating an effective volunteer program and maintaining open communication are also important steps to ensure the success of your charity.*

Chapter 11
Evaluating Your Progress

In the late 2010s, much was made of the new trend of 'data-driven decision-making'. Companies, organisations, and governments all over the world were scrambling to collect data, analyse it with AI, and use it to make informed decisions. Although this is a great way to solve complex problems, your charity has another powerful tool at its disposal: evaluation.

Think of it this way: You're walking in a jungle and you want to get to the other side. You can take the easy route and hope for the best, or you can stop and take a look around at your progress. Doing this will give you an idea of where you are in relation to where you're going, what areas need attention, and whether there are any hidden dangers (or opportunities!) waiting for you further down the path.

The same principles apply when evaluating your charity's progress. By monitoring and assessing how your programs are performing, collecting data from stakeholders, implementing program evaluation techniques, and measuring outcomes—all of which we'll discuss later—you'll be able to make informed decisions about the future of your organisation.

It's essential to view every investment and intervention as a project. A project would, minimally, have a beginning and an end. Projects are crafted and launched for specific reasons with the intent to deliver change. For this reason, they are temporal—with an agreed time, cost, and scope. Clarity is expected. It's important to provide convincing methodology and steps on how the project will achieve a clear overall goal (impact level), strategic objectives, outcomes, and outputs, as well as clearly state the activities that will be undertaken and the inputs (both financial or human) needed to accomplish the task.

In our contemporary world, projects are about delivering benefits (change), just as businesses are about profit. A project should seek a triple bottom line of social, economic, and environmental benefits.

Not only that but by regularly monitoring and assessing your progress, you'll be able to identify areas of strength and weakness, pinpoint problems before they become too big to solve and develop strategies to reach your goals more efficiently. With the right tools in place—and some savvy analysis—evaluating your charity's progress can help ensure you remain on track for success.

Monitoring and Evaluation

Monitoring and evaluation (M&E) are two key elements of any charity's success. Monitoring is the process of collecting data that will enable you to assess the performance of your programs, whereas evaluation looks at how effective those programs have been in achieving their intended purpose.

An important aspect you would need to keep your eyes on (and a major preoccupation of your M&E staff) is how well your set of activities are resulting in output, outcomes and ultimately impact. This will also need you to consider and constantly review the possible factors that may impact (positively or negatively) your project goal.

This linear presentation is often referred to as Impact Chain.

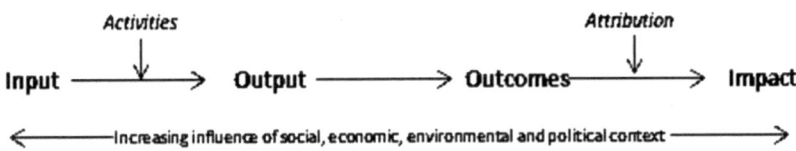

Figure 2: Impact Chain

An example of how the impact chain is used in an education project is provided below:

Impact ↑	-Food and better nutrition -Increase employment opportunities -Higher literacy rate among girl children -improved health;
Outcomes ↑	-Increase yield per acre. Increased income. Crop diversity increased -Higher completion of school by girls (Retention) -Improved clean drinking water supply -Open defaecation reduced
Output ↑	-Farmers Trained; Size of Land Cultivated (in acres); Farm inputs (tools, seeds, fertilizers) supplied; Farmers trained in improved agronomic practices and small traders trained in financial literacy, -Female Teacher Trained; Schools Built; School Materials Supplied; -Water Wells Constructed, Water Well Maintenance Technicians Trained, Water Well Chlorinated Safe for Drinking, Water Pumps Installed, Improved Toilet Constructed. Awareness Raising on Hygiene Conducted.
Inputs ↑	Funds mobilised for the project Staff recruited and deployed Materials purchased to execute the project (Financial and human resources)

Figure 3: Simple impact chain for an integrated agriculture, education and health program
Source: Concern Worldwide

It's important to set up a system for monitoring and evaluating your progress on an ongoing basis—this can be done through surveys, interviews, questionnaires, or other data collection methods. The data should then be analysed regularly to help identify areas for improvement and inform future decisions about your organisation's goals and strategies.

Data Collection

The first step in monitoring and evaluating your progress is collecting data from stakeholders (e.g., donors, volunteers, beneficiaries), as well as other sources (e.g., research studies, and government reports). The data should include both quantitative and qualitative information. Quantitative data are often easier to analyse but can be limited in scope, whereas qualitative data can give you a more detailed understanding of how people think and feel about your organisation's programs and project initiatives.

A good data collection system has some major traits that separate it from the rest. The following list provides a few guidelines for setting up your data collection system:

- *Identify the types of data you need to collect.*
- *Develop a strategy for collecting and storing that data.*
- *Ensure the data collected are accurate, complete, and up-to-date.*
- *Create procedures for regularly reviewing and verifying the data.*
- *Securely store all collected information.*

Oftentimes, bogus data can be more dangerous than no data at all. Make sure your data collection system is accurate and reliable so you can make informed decisions based on it. To make sure your data are reliable, you should also regularly audit it and look for signs of bias or inaccuracy.

Key Steps in Developing and Implementing an M&E Plan

1. Conduct team and stakeholder consultation.
2. Define the process for stakeholder involvement.
3. Translate the problem statement, program goals, and objectives into M&E frameworks.
4. Establish the scope of the M&E plan.
5. Develop the M&E framework.
6. Determine the elements to be monitored and evaluated.
7. Define the indicators and identify the data sources.
8. Determine the M&E methods for data and information collection.
9. Develop the data collection plan.
10. Determine the M&E responsibilities.
11. Set targets.
12. Define the reporting system, utilisation, and dissemination of results.
13. Plan for mid-course adjustments.

Data Collection Plan

Start with a consultative process with your team and key stakeholders to ensure the data collection exercise is all-inclusive. In your data collection plan, consider the following:

- Indicators to measure
- Who is responsible
- Timing
- Data quality notes

We found it's important to also consider from the outset how and who is going to analyse the data you collect. This may also extend to knowing who's going to write up the report in such a way that's concise and provides useful information.

The set of questions to ask during the consultation sessions could include the following:

- Who'll be responsible for data collection and its supervision?
- Who'll be responsible for ensuring data quality at each stage?
- How will data quality be checked at every stage?
- How often will the data be collected, compiled, sent, and analysed?
- What indicators will be derived from each data source?
- How will the data be sent (raw, summary)?
- What tools/forms will be used, if any?
- What resources (e.g., staff, office supplies, computers, transportation) will be needed at each stage?
- Who'll analyse the data? How often will the analysis occur?
- How often will the results be compiled into reports?
- To whom and how often will the results be disseminated?

Old school pen and paper are still trusted and are largely in use, but the use of digital data collection tools is gaining popularity among M&E practitioners. A few relevant software programs include Kobo, Survey Monkey, and CommCare.

Key Takeaways

1. Start early.
2. Involve stakeholders at all stages in the data collection process.
3. Assess the strategic information needs of intended users.
4. Assess current capacity and use what's already available.
5. Avoid duplication of data collection and reporting.
6. Don't collect information that will not be used.

- Review progress/results regularly and make adjustments to the M&E plan, if necessary.

Data Analysis

Once you've collected your data, the next step is to analyse it to better understand what it means and how it can help inform decisions about your organisation's programs and initiatives. This can be done through a variety of methods, such as statistical analysis, qualitative research, or predictive analytics.

The type of analysis used will depend on the type of data being analysed and the intended purpose. For example, if you're trying to identify trends or patterns in donor behaviour, then using predictive analytics may be more effective than conducting a survey.

It's also important to consider which tools (e.g., Excel, SPSS) and techniques (e.g., regression analysis, statistical tests) will be most suitable for the type of data being analysed.

So how does one analyse data properly? The following list provides a few guidelines for data analysis:

- Understand the goal of your analysis.
- Determine which data are most relevant to achieving that goal.
- Choose appropriate tools and techniques to analyse the data.
- Review the results of your analysis and make any necessary changes or adjustments.
- Present the results in an easy-to-understand format.

Program Evaluation

KPIs and metrics are useful for monitoring your progress but they don't tell the whole story. Ultimately, what matters most is how successful your charity is in achieving its mission and goals. Program evaluation helps you understand how effective your programs and services are in meeting those objectives.

Program evaluation involves measuring outcomes against established standards or baselines to determine whether a program has achieved its desired results. It also looks at factors such as return on investment (ROI) and cost-effectiveness. This type of evaluation requires having an effective data collection system to accurately measure progress and success over time.

Let's say you're working on a school-based program focusing on student literacy. You can collect data on student academic performance before and after the program, then measure these results against established baselines to determine whether the program is meeting its goals.

Outcomes Measurement

The final step in evaluating progress is measuring outcomes. Outcome measurement looks at how well an organisation or program has achieved its predetermined goals and objectives. This involves collecting data on activities (e.g., number of people served, number of resources utilised), as well as assessing impact (e.g., changes in behaviour, attitudes, and skills).

This type of evaluation requires long-term monitoring and analysis to ensure the desired results are being achieved over time. It's important to collect data on both short- and long-term outcomes to effectively assess the success of a program or initiative.

Lean Data Monitoring and Evaluation Team

Throughout the process of evaluating your progress, it's important to have a dedicated team in place that's focused on monitoring and evaluation. This team should be responsible for designing data collection systems, analysing and interpreting data, conducting program evaluations, and measuring outcomes.

It's also helpful to have a Lean Data Monitoring and Evaluation Team that meets regularly to discuss progress on projects and initiatives. Having an established system of regular meetings helps ensure everyone stays informed about the status of programs and activities so the necessary adjustments can be made, as needed. While the technical discussions should be left to the team, a senior-level leader should be involved in monitoring and evaluating program outcomes. This helps ensure the organisation remains focused on achieving its mission and goals.

Extracting the Best Outcome

The data will show a lot of areas where your charity can improve but it will also show areas where you've been successful and should continue doing what you're doing. Knowing which outcome to pursue or replicate is key to any charity's success.

The following five tips can help you in evaluating your progress and getting the best outcome from your data:

1. *Sharing of metrics across the board*: Regularly compare your metrics with similar charities and look for areas where you can learn from them. Doing this will help you stay ahead of the curve and maximise your impact.
2. *Standardising evaluation tools*: Establish and utilise standard evaluation tools so all data can be easily compared and interpreted. This will ensure you have accurate results and reliable insights.
3. *Invest in training*: Make sure your team has the right skills to analyse the data collected. Regular training sessions on data analysis techniques such as regression, correlation, and so on will help your charity's staff get better equipped to make informed decisions based on data.
4. *Learn from painful lessons*: Take the time to analyse data from unsuccessful initiatives. This will help you identify areas for improvement and learn from mistakes.
5. *Feedback loops*: Set up a system to collect feedback from stakeholders and beneficiaries. This will help you identify areas of improvement in your programs, as well as receive insights into how people feel about the charity.

Evaluating your progress should be an integral part of running any charity. Regularly tracking metrics, analysing data, and gathering feedback are key steps in ensuring your program's success.

Key Takeaways

- *Monitoring and evaluation are essential to tracking the progress of your charity.*
- *Choose appropriate tools and techniques for analysing the data.*
- *Program evaluations measure outcomes against established baselines.*
- *Outcome measurement looks at how well an organisation or program has achieved predetermined goals and objectives.*
- *Collect feedback from stakeholders and beneficiaries to obtain a better understanding of your charity's performance.*
- *Learn from past mistakes and analyse data from unsuccessful initiatives. This will help you identify areas for improvement.*

Chapter 12
Weathering the Storm

It's a reality that there will be testing times while on the journey to reaching your charity's goals. It's essential to be prepared for when a challenge arises, no matter how big or small it may be. Weathering the storm will require risk management and crisis management skills, as well as an understanding of change management, adversity, emergency standard operating procedures (SOPs), and business continuity planning.

Imagine a situation where, all of a sudden, a major funding source for your charity is taken away. How will you respond? Will you be able to continue to provide the services that were being offered? It's important to think through these types of scenarios and have a plan in place so that, if and when they happen; there will not be an interruption to what you're doing.

In this chapter, we'll explore different strategies to help you manage risk and respond to crises. We'll discuss the importance of having emergency SOPs in place, as well as ideas for developing business continuity plans. Lastly, we'll talk about how to stay positive and resilient when faced with adversity so your charity remains strong throughout any difficulties it may face.

What is Weathering the Storm?

Everyone has experienced a storm in one form or another. Whether it be the economic downturn of 2020, starting a business, or a devastating natural disaster, there's no doubt weathering storms can take a toll on us. But what does it really mean to 'weather the storm'? What are some of the strategies and techniques we can use to come out on top when it seems like all hope is lost? Let's commence exploring just that. Here, we'll discuss what it takes to survive difficult times and come out stronger on the other side. Read on to discover tips and tactics for weathering any storm life throws your way!

The Types of Weathering

Basic geography teaches that *weathering* is the process of breaking down rock, soil, and minerals into smaller pieces. There are two types of weathering: physical and chemical.

Physical weathering happens when rocks are broken down by the forces of wind, water, ice, and heat. This type of weathering doesn't change the chemical makeup of the rocks.

Chemical weathering happens when rocks are changed chemically. This can happen when rainwater seeps into rocks and changes their composition or when acid rain falls on rocks and dissolves them.

The Causes of Weathering

Weathering the storm can have many causes. Some of the most common include high winds, heavy rain, flooding, and lightning. Although these are all natural causes of weathering, there are also man-made causes. Construction activity, for example, can create dust and dirt that can be blown around by the wind and cause weathering. Vehicle traffic can also generate dust and dirt that can lead to weathering.

Weathering the storm is not an easy task but it can be done if you stay focused on your goal and look for ways to cope with the difficulties that come along. It's important to remember, that no matter how tough times may be, there'll always be a light at the end of the tunnel. Even in our darkest moments, we need to keep faith and hope alive because those are essential tools for surviving what life throws at us. With resilience and perseverance, we can weather any storm!

Weathering the storm, therefore, refers to the process of enduring a difficult or challenging situation. It's often used as a metaphor for overcoming adversity. Weathering the storm requires strength, perseverance, and resilience. It's not easy but it's possible. When we weather the storm, we learn and grow from the experience. We become stronger and more capable of handling whatever life throws our way.

The best time to weather a storm is when you're prepared for it. This means having a plan in place and being ready to implement it when the time comes. It also means knowing your limits and being realistic about what you can and cannot handle.

Starting to weather the storm when you're not prepared can be disastrous. You may find yourself scrambling to put together a plan at the last minute, which can lead to mistakes being made. Additionally, if you try to take on more than you can realistically handle, you'll only end up burning yourself out and making the situation worse.

If at all possible, try to start weathering the storm before it hits. This gives you time to get your ducks in a row and ensures you're as prepared as possible. Once the storm hits, it'll be too late to make any changes or adjustments, so it's important you have everything in place beforehand.

Of course, sometimes storms come out of nowhere, and there's no way to prepare for them.

How to Weather a Storm

To weather a storm, it's important to have a plan and be prepared. Here are some tips on how to weather a storm:

1. *Know the risks.* Be sure to check the forecast and know what types of storms are expected. This will help you plan and be prepared for the worst.
2. *Have a plan.* Having a plan will help you stay safe and know what to do in case of an emergency.
3. *Be prepared.* Make sure you have everything you need in case of an emergency, such as food, water, and first-aid supplies.
4. *Stay indoors.* When a storm is raging, it's best to stay indoors where it's safe. If you must go outside, be sure to wear proper clothing and footwear to protect yourself from the elements.
5. *Stay calm.* Storms can be scary, but it's important to stay calm and focused to weather the storm safely.

We've explored what it means to weather the storm and how this can be an invaluable tool in times of difficulty. Weathering the storm takes fortitude, resilience, and a commitment to remaining focused on a long-term goal, despite the obstacles that may arise along the way. By taking things one step at a time, we can come out of our storms with newfound strength and perspective, allowing us to thrive even further than before our adversity.

Risk Management

A risk is an uncertain event or set of events that, should it occur, will have an effect on the achievement of objectives.

- Risk is measured by the combination of the probability of a perceived threat or opportunity occurring and the magnitude of its impact on objectives.
- The impact on the objectives can be measured by using KPIs (Key performance Indicators).

KPI is a measure of performance that is used to help an organisation define and evaluate how successful it is in making progress towards its organisational objectives.

- A threat could be viewed as a negative risk.
- Opportunities could also be viewed as a positive risk.

Risk management is the process of identifying, analysing, and addressing the potential risks that may affect an organisation. It involves identifying the potential risks organisations may face, evaluating the likelihood and potential impact of those risks, and implementing strategies to mitigate or eliminate those risks. This process is critical for organisations of all sizes because it helps ensure the long-term stability and success of the organisation. The five essential steps of a Risk Management Process are: i) Identify the Risk, ii) Analyse the Risk, iii) Evaluate or Rank the Risk, iv) Treat the Risk and v) Monitor and Review the Risk.

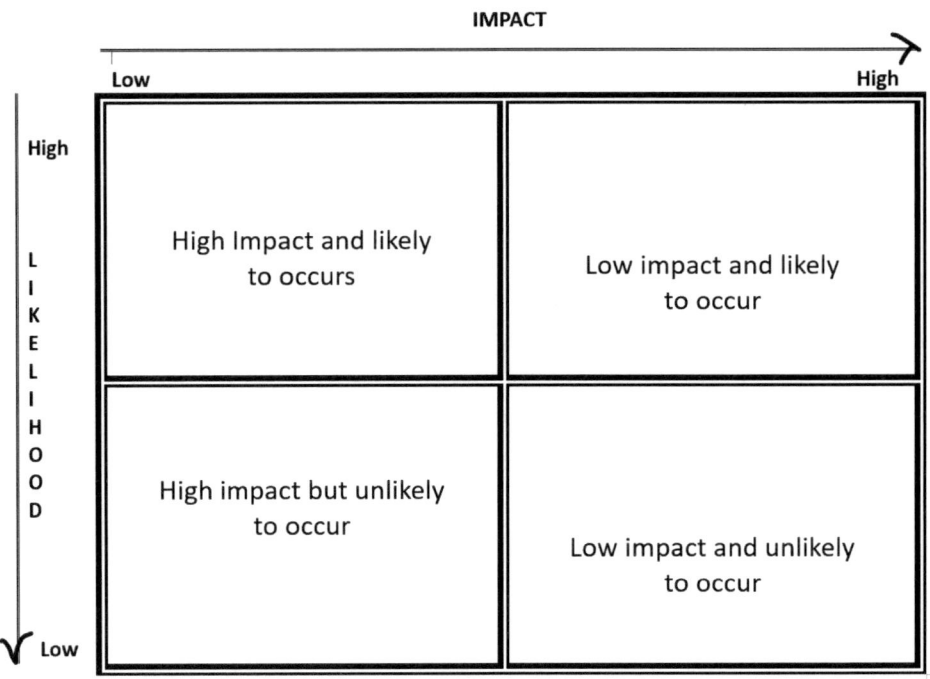

Barua, Suborna & Kar, Dipon & Mahbub, Fariza. (2018).

There are several key components to effective risk management. The first step is identifying the risks an organisation or your project may face. This can be done through a variety of methods, including analysing historical data, conducting a SWOT analysis, and engaging in scenario planning. It's important to consider both internal and external risks and short- and long-term risks.

Once risks have been identified, the next step is to evaluate the likelihood and potential impact of those risks. This involves analysing the potential consequences of each risk, as well as the likelihood of it occurring. This can be done through a variety of methods, including risk assessments and probability analyses.

Once the risks have been identified and evaluated, the next step is to implement strategies to mitigate or eliminate those risks. This can include a variety of tactics, such as implementing risk control measures, transferring risks through insurance or other risk transfer mechanisms, and establishing contingency plans in case the risk does occur.

There are several key benefits to effective risk management. First and foremost, it helps protect organisations from potential losses or damages. By identifying and addressing potential risks, organisations can minimise the impact of risk on their operations and financial stability. Additionally, effective risk management can help build trust and confidence with stakeholders, such as customers, employees, and shareholders. This is especially important in today's business environment, where organisations are increasingly expected to be transparent and accountable for their actions.

Effective risk management also helps to improve decision-making within organisations. By considering the potential risks and consequences of a decision, organisations can make more informed and strategic decisions that are better aligned with their long-term goals and objectives. This can help minimise the impact of negative events on the organisation and increase its overall resilience.

There are several key considerations that organisations should take into account when implementing a risk management program. The first is to ensure the program is aligned with the overall goals and objectives of the organisation. This includes identifying the specific risks that are most relevant to the organisation and developing strategies tailored to those risks. Most organisations have a strategic plan. This is a useful document that guides the operation of the organisation and often spells out the scope of what you intend to do and the extent of accomplishment envisaged within a period of time. Three-to-five-year strategic plans are very common among humanitarian organisations.

Another key consideration is ensuring the risk management program is integrated into the overall operations of the organisation. This includes training employees on risk management principles and practices, as well as establishing processes and procedures to ensure risks are identified and addressed in a timely and effective manner.

In addition, it's important to regularly review and update the risk management program to ensure its effective and relevant. This includes conducting periodic risk assessments and reviewing the performance of the program on an ongoing basis.

There are several key challenges that organisations may face when implementing a risk management program. One of the biggest challenges is the need to balance the cost of implementing risk management measures with the potential benefits. This can be difficult because it may not always be clear what the long-term consequences of a particular risk will be. Additionally, organisations may struggle to get buy-in from employees or stakeholders for certain risk management measures, especially if those measures require significant changes to the way the organisation operates or are influenced by the policies of the host government.

Another challenge is the need to constantly monitor and review risks. As the business environment changes, the risks faced by an organisation may change as well. This requires ongoing vigilance and the ability to adapt the risk management program as needed.

The old saying goes, 'It's not a matter of if something bad will happen, but when'.

When you're leading a charity, it's especially important to plan ahead and be prepared for potential threats. Risk management is an essential part of running any organisation, and as the founder or leader of your charity, you should have a comprehensive risk assessment ready that identifies areas of vulnerability and helps you decide how best to deal with them.

Risk management involves being proactive rather than reactive. It means recognising what could go wrong before it does and having plans in place for each possible scenario. Consider creating policies for different types of risks that cover everything from financial catastrophes to natural disasters, cyber-attacks, and communications glitches. Risk management also includes seizing the opportunity that may arise. Thus, where others see problems, you may see opportunities.

By taking a proactive approach to risk management, you may be able to avoid or mitigate some crises that could otherwise put your charity's work in jeopardy. Every organisation should have an emergency response plan in place so everyone knows what to do if something goes wrong. This plan should include steps for communication, mobilisation of resources, and decision-making procedures.

Finally, create a framework for evaluating risks on an ongoing basis—this will help you keep track of potential threats and ensure you're ready to respond quickly if something does happen. With the right preparation and planning, you can weather any storm!

Crisis Management

A crisis in a charity can take the shape of multiple things, from a sudden drop in donations to a natural disaster that affects the service you provide. No matter what form it takes, the impact can be huge on the charity, its employees, and volunteers—and even donors.

Crisis management is a critical aspect of any organisation's operations because it involves the actions taken to prevent or mitigate the impact of crises on organisations and their stakeholders. Crises can be defined as unexpected and potentially dangerous or damaging events that require immediate attention and action to prevent further harm. They can be triggered by various factors such as natural disasters, accidents, financial problems, or even pandemics.

Effective crisis management involves planning, communication, and coordination to ensure organisations are prepared to handle crises and minimise their impact. It's crucial for organisations to have a crisis management plan in place to guide their actions and decision-making in the event of crises. This plan should include steps to identify potential crises, assess the risks, develop strategies to mitigate the impact and communicate with stakeholders.

The first step in crisis management is identifying the potential crises that could affect the organisation. This involves identifying the potential risks and hazards that could occur, as well as assessing the likelihood of these events occurring and the potential impact they could have on the organisation. It's essential to have a comprehensive list of potential crises that could affect the organisation, as well as a plan to monitor and assess these risks on an ongoing basis.

Once the potential crises have been identified, the organisation needs to develop strategies to mitigate their impact. This may involve implementing preventative measures to reduce the likelihood of a crisis occurring, such as improving safety protocols or strengthening financial controls. It may also involve developing contingency plans to address the consequences of a crisis if it does occur. For example, if a natural disaster were to occur, organisations might have plans in place to evacuate employees and secure critical infrastructure.

Effective communication is a crucial aspect of crisis management because it allows organisations to keep stakeholders informed and provide guidance on how to respond to the crisis. This includes not only internal stakeholders such as employees but also external stakeholders such as customers, suppliers, and the media. It's essential for organisations to have a communication plan in place outlining the channels and methods they'll use to communicate with stakeholders during crises. This may involve using social media, emails, or press releases to provide updates and instructions.

Coordination is another essential component of crisis management because it involves coordinating the efforts of various stakeholders to effectively respond to crises. This may involve working with government agencies, emergency services, and other organisations to provide support and resources. It's essential for organisations to have a clear chain of command and designated roles and responsibilities to ensure everyone knows their part in the crisis management plan.

In the event of a crisis, organisations should also be prepared to review and assess their response efforts and make any necessary adjustments. This may involve conducting post-crises reviews to identify any areas for improvement and ensuring the organisation is better prepared for future crises.

One of the most challenging aspects of crisis management is managing the impact on stakeholders, such as providing support and assistance to employees who have been affected by the crisis, as well as communicating with customers and other external stakeholders to reassure them and provide information about the steps being taken to address the crisis.

Effective crisis management also involves maintaining transparency and honesty in communication. This means being open and transparent about the situation and any challenges the organisation is facing, as well as providing accurate and timely updates to stakeholders. It's essential to avoid downplaying the impact of the crisis or providing false information because this can erode trust and damage the organisation's reputation.

It's essential for organisations to have a crisis management plan in place to guide their actions and decision-making in the event of crises. This plan should include steps to identify potential crises, assess the risks, and develop strategies to mitigate them. It should include how to prepare for crises, who will take charge in crisis situations, step-by-step procedures outlining how to handle each type of crisis, and guidelines on keeping communication open with stakeholders throughout.

The point is to prioritise safety and be prepared to take decisive action. The plan should include how the organisation will respond, what resources need to be mobilised, and any steps necessary to minimise damage. It's also important to have a system in place for monitoring and tracking incidents as they occur so you can update your crisis management plan accordingly.

The Pareto's principle can be useful here: The idea is that eighty per cent of your results come from twenty per cent of your effort, so focus on the essential elements that will help you weather any crisis. With a well-thought-out plan in place, you can be confident your charity is prepared for anything.

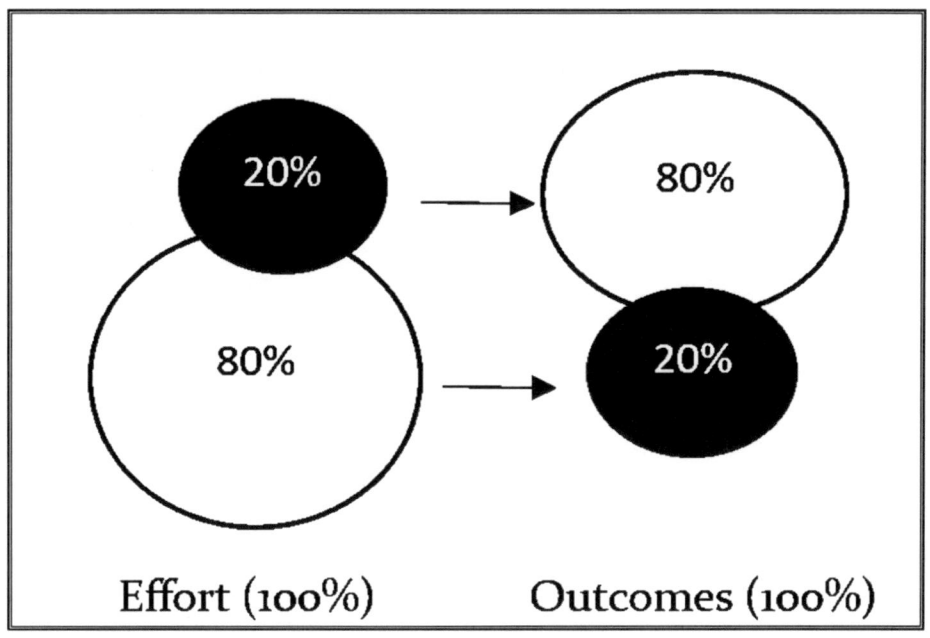

Figure 4: The Pareto's 80:20 Principle
Source: Laoyan 2022

Change Management

Change is inevitable—it's a fact of life when running a charity. New technologies, new laws, changing social dynamics—all of these things can affect the way your organisation operates and how it provides services to its constituents. In charity work, it may also mean change in the circumstances and situations previously prioritised. Suppose you choose to support countries in the least developed category, well your organisation and project objectives may change if the situation in the country over time improves. It may mean you'd have to redirect your support to other countries or projects where support is more needed.

Managing that process is crucial to the senior management, mid-level management, staff and volunteers, and the beneficiaries. You may have to say goodbye to people who still believe they clearly have a need because the operating environment and donor landscape have changed.

Change management is the process of implementing and managing change within an organisation. It involves identifying the need for change, analysing the current state of the organisation, planning and implementing the changes, and evaluating the results.

There are many different approaches to change management but the most common is the Kotter model, developed by John Kotter in the 1980s. This model consists of eight steps: establishing a sense of urgency, forming a coalition, creating a vision, communicating the vision, empowering others to act on the vision, creating short-term wins, consolidating gains and producing more change, and anchoring new approaches in the company's culture.

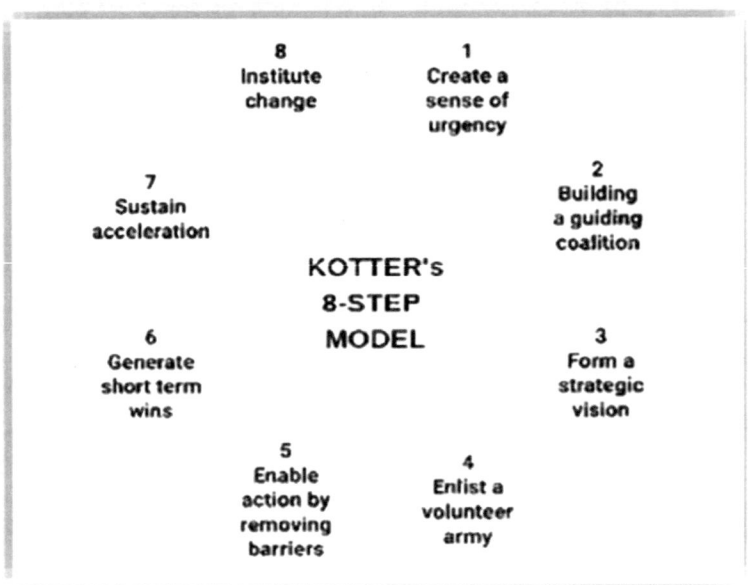

Figure 5: Koters Model of Change Management

One of the key elements of successful change management is effective communication. It's essential to clearly communicate the reasons for the change, the benefits of the change, and the steps that will be taken to implement the change. This helps ensure all stakeholders are on board with the change and are able to support it.

Another important aspect of change management is stakeholder management. This involves identifying all stakeholders affected by the change, including employees, customers, suppliers, and shareholders, and ensuring their needs and concerns are taken into account during the change process.

Effective change management also requires strong leadership. This includes setting a clear vision for the change, providing support and resources to those implementing the change, and creating a culture of continuous improvement within the organisation.

One of the main challenges of change management is resistance to change. This can occur at all levels of an organisation, from employees to senior management. It's important to anticipate and address potential resistance to change because this can help ensure the success of the change process.

There are a number of strategies that can be used to manage resistance to change, including the following:

- Communicating the reasons for the change and the benefits it will bring.
- Involving employees in the change process and giving them a sense of ownership.
- Providing training and support to help employees adapt to the change.
- Addressing any concerns or fears employees may have about the change.

Change management is a continuous process because organisations are constantly evolving and adapting to new circumstances. It's important to regularly review and assess the effectiveness of the change process and make any necessary adjustments to ensure the organisation remains agile and able to respond to new challenges and opportunities.

One key tool that can be used in the change management process is having a change management plan. This is a document outlining the steps that will be taken to implement the change, the resources that will be required, and the key stakeholders involved. It should also include a timeline for the change process and a budget.

The change management plan should be communicated to all stakeholders, including employees, customers, and suppliers, to ensure everyone is aware of the changes being made and how they'll be affected.

Another important aspect of change management is risk management. This involves identifying any potential risks associated with the change and developing a plan to mitigate those risks. This could include contingency plans in case the change does not go as planned or measures to ensure the change is implemented smoothly and without any disruption to the business.

Change management is essential for organisations looking to grow and adapt to new circumstances. By implementing a structured change management process, organisations can ensure change is managed effectively and that the benefits of the change are realised. It's important to have strategies in place for managing change and staying ahead of the curve. That means being open to embracing new ideas and processes while also maintaining existing ones. Consider setting up an internal change team who'll be responsible for leading change initiatives within the organisation and developing the best strategies for dealing with change.

You should also consider creating a culture of continuous learning so everyone in the organisation is constantly evolving and growing. This could include offering training courses and workshops, encouraging open dialogue about new ideas, or even hiring external consultants to help brainstorm solutions to challenges.

By staying agile and adapting quickly to changes as they come up, your charity can continue on its trajectory of growth and success—even when the winds of change are blowing strong.

Dealing with Adversity

Adversity is an all-too-familiar part of life for charities. Whether it's financial difficulties, a difficult donor relationship, or criticism from stakeholders—sometimes things don't go as planned. Adversity is a natural part of life. It can come in many forms, such as a financial setback, a health crisis, a relationship breakdown, or a natural disaster. No one is immune to adversity and it's something we all must deal with at some point in our lives.

Dealing with adversity can be incredibly challenging and overwhelming, and it's natural to feel angry, frustrated, and helpless in the face of it. However, it's important to remember adversity is not a permanent state and that there are things we can do to cope with it and come out stronger on the other side.

One of the most important things to remember when dealing with adversity is to take care of yourself. This means taking time to rest and recharge, getting enough sleep, eating well, and finding ways to relax and de-stress. It's also important to reach out for support when you need it. This can be in the form of talking to a friend or family member, seeking therapy, or joining a support group.

Also vital is finding ways to stay positive and focus on the things going well in your life. This can be difficult when you're facing adversity but it's important to try to maintain a positive outlook and find things to be grateful for. This can help you feel more resilient and better able to cope with the challenges you're facing.

Another important aspect of dealing with adversity is finding ways to take action. This can involve seeking out resources and support, making a plan, and taking small steps towards overcoming the challenges you're facing. It's also important to be patient and remember progress takes time.

One way to take action is by setting goals for yourself. This can help you stay focused and motivated and feel a sense of accomplishment as you make progress. It's also important to be flexible and adjust your goals, as needed, as the circumstances of your adversity may change over time.

It's also important to remember adversity can be a source of growth and learning. Although it can be difficult to see at the time, adversity can help us develop new skills and strengths and learn more about ourselves and our capabilities. It can also help us build resilience and become more resilient in the face of future challenges.

Finally, it's important to be kind to yourself when dealing with adversity. It's easy to be hard on yourself and to feel like you should be able to handle everything on your own, but you must remember it's okay to ask for help and to take care of yourself.

In conclusion, dealing with adversity can be challenging but it's something we all must do at some point in our lives. By taking care of ourselves, maintaining a positive outlook, taking action, and being kind to ourselves, we can learn to cope with adversity and come out stronger on the other side.

When adversity strikes, it's critical to maintain a positive attitude and try to stay focused on the charity's long-term goals. That means having a plan in place for how you'll respond to any given situation and being willing to make changes, if necessary. It also means looking for ways to turn lemons into lemonade—learning from mistakes and coming up with creative solutions that can help the organisation move forward.

Adversity is not something we can avoid but it's something we can learn from. By recognising what went wrong and taking steps to ensure it doesn't happen again, your charity can remain resilient in the face of challenges and continue its mission.

Charities or organisations function similarly to the human body—the system can only be as strong as its weakest link.

Therefore, we must continue to build on our strengths and shore up any weak links. Doing so will ensure we're better prepared for whatever storm may come our way—both expected and unexpected. With an effective risk management plan in place, crisis management protocol established, change management strategies implemented, and a positive attitude towards adversity, there's no challenge too big for the charity to tackle. Weathering the storm takes focus and dedication, but with the right preparation, even the toughest storms can be overcome.

Key Takeaways

- *Establish a comprehensive risk assessment for your charity.*
- *Create emergency SOPs to prepare for potential threats.*
- *Stay positive and resilient in the face of adversity.*
- *Embrace change and create a culture of learning.*
- *Adopt an attitude that fosters a growth mindset and continuous improvement.*

Chapter 13
Measuring Impact and Success

If you recall, the project life cycle starts with initiation, followed by planning, executing, and closing, whereas monitoring and evaluation runs through every stage. When it comes to measuring impact, there are a few key ways you can get a better understanding of whether or not your mission is being fulfilled. First and foremost, it's important to set a baseline: where was the recipient before your donation? How do they stand now? What has changed over time as a result of your efforts?

> Impact: The fruit of any fundraising effort. The goal of the game.

If you're a business, it can be hard to measure your impact and success. How do you determine whether what you're doing is really making an impact or if the investments you're making are paying off in terms of success? Together let's explore how to measure impact and success from different perspectives, including financial performance, customer satisfaction, employee engagement, and more. We'll discuss different methods of measuring these metrics and provide tips on how to determine which method is best for your business. Read on to learn more about measuring impact and success!

What is Impact?

In its simplest terms, the impact is the difference you make in the world. When you're trying to make an impact, what you're really doing is trying to create positive change.

The European Union has developed a very simple evaluation framework (below) that helps explain what to consider when measuring the impact of your charity investment. This is also known as DAC Criteria. Impact is a high-level evaluation criterion along the impact chain and should be viewed along with the other core five: relevance, effectiveness, coherence, efficiency, and sustainability.

There are a lot of ways to measure impact. You can look at how many people you've helped, how much money you've raised, how many lives you've touched—but, ultimately, it comes down to how much difference you've made. Let's take a look at the way the many donors such as the European Union explain the evaluation criteria (see the figure inserted below). This is viewed and used as a framework for evaluation by many M&E and project management practitioners.

Figure 6: OECD DAC Criteria

Some people focus on making a big impact in a short amount of time. Others focus on making a smaller impact that lasts long term. There isn't necessarily a right or wrong way to do it—it all depends on what works best for you and your goals.

The important thing is you remain intentional about making an impact. It's not enough to just do good things—you need to be purposeful and strategic about it if you want to see real change in the world.

What is Success?

There's no single answer to the question of what success looks like because it depends on each individual's goals and aspirations. However, some general qualities are often associated with success, such as happiness, a sense of accomplishment, and feeling proud of what you've achieved.

In project management, to measure your own success, it's important to first identify what your goals are or the expected requirements of your client, establish the baselines, set a target of achievement of change, and then track your progress towards achieving them. This can be done by setting regular milestones and celebrating (ticking off) each time you reach one. Check the change in the baseline level of your target beneficiaries over the period. Additionally, it's helpful to get feedback from others to obtain an objective perspective on your progress.

Ultimately, success is a personal journey that looks different for everyone and an endeavour that brings about change within scope, cost, and time. By definition, it means achieving something you've set out to do within the period you predetermined and within budget. So as long as you're moving closer towards your goals and making progress, you can consider yourself to be on the path to being successful!

The key parameters to consider when measuring the success of your charity begin with measuring how your resources and activities were used to undertake an activity that produced an output, followed by an outcome and then a measure of the impact of your investment. A cliché I found useful when deploying this is to ask myself 'And so what?'. Measuring this interrelationship (along the impact chain) is popular among humanitarian practitioners, and the criteria developed by the OECD, known as the DAC Criteria for project monitoring and evaluation, are among the most popular. The definitions of the elements that make up the DAC Criteria (i.e., relevance, effectiveness, efficiency, coherence, sustainability, and impact) are presented below:

Relevance

Relevance is about whether the intervention is *doing the right thing*.

This is the extent to which the intervention objectives and design respond to beneficiaries'* global, country, and partner/institution needs, policies, and priorities—and continue to do so (adapting) if circumstances change.

Note, 'Respond to' means the objectives and design of the intervention are sensitive to the economic, environmental, equity, social, political economy, and capacity conditions in which they take place. 'Partner/institution' includes the governments (national, regional, local), civil society organisations, private entities, and international bodies involved in funding, implementing, and/or overseeing the intervention. Relevance assessment involves looking at differences and trade-offs between priorities or needs. It requires analysing any changes in the context to assess the extent to which the intervention can be (or has been) adapted to remain relevant.

*Beneficiaries are defined as 'the individuals, groups, or organisations, whether targeted or not, that benefit directly or indirectly from the development intervention'. Other terms, such as rights holders, participants, persons of concern, or affected people, may also be used. I heard someone, for instance, saying the use of 'beneficiary' is a bit demeaning if not patronising. Another participant in a workshop said the connotation of 'beneficiary' makes the power relationship between the giver and the receiver skewed too much in favour of the receiver.

Coherence

Coherence speaks to *how well the intervention fits.* In other words, it asks about the compatibility of the intervention with other interventions in a country, sector, or institution. This would also check the extent to which other interventions (particularly policies) support or undermine the intervention, and vice versa.

It's often a good practice in the analysis of coherence to look at it from both internal coherence and external coherence.

- Internal coherence would address the synergies and interlinkages between the intervention and other interventions carried out by the same institution/government, as well as the consistency of the intervention with the relevant international norms and standards to which that institution/government adheres.
- External coherence considers the consistency of the intervention with other actors' interventions in the same context. This includes complementarity, harmonisation, and coordination with others, as well

as the extent to which the intervention is adding value while avoiding duplication of effort.

Effectiveness

This is about whether an intervention is *achieving its objectives.*

This area of evaluation measures the extent to which the intervention achieved, or is expected to achieve, its objectives and results, including any differential results across groups. The analysis of effectiveness involves taking account of the relative importance of the objectives or results.

Efficiency

How well are *resources being used?*

Efficiency is about the extent to which the intervention delivers, or is likely to deliver, results in an economic and timely way. In this case, 'Economic' is the measure of and analysis of how the intervention measures the conversion of inputs (funds, expertise, natural resources, time, etc.) into outputs, outcomes, and impacts in the most cost-effective way possible compared to feasible alternatives. The term 'value for money' has been used and requested by some donors as an analysis point to determine efficiency.

Calculating the value for money in humanitarian projects can be complex yet very necessary. According to DFID Evaluation Report EV 645, by Derek Poate and Christopher Barnett (2003), on Measuring Value for Money, the indicator is measured as the percentage of projects rated one or two on a scale of five. It is calculated in three separate classes for projects classified by high, medium or low risk status. For example:

$$\frac{\text{Total commitment value of high-risk projects approved at Director level and above, scoring 1 or 2}}{\text{Total commitment value of all high-risk projects approved at Director level 15 and above (excluding those scoring x)}}$$

They suggested rating scores and risk categories as shown in the box below:

Achievement Rating	Achievement

The following rating scheme should be used to rate the likelihood of achieving outputs and in turn, fulfilling the project's purpose.
   1   = likely to be completely achieved
   2   = likely to be largely achieved
   3   = likely to be partially achieved
   4   = only likely to be achieved to a very limited extent
   5   = unlikely to be realised x = too early to judge the extent of achievement
	Projects can be categorised into one of three categories of risk as follows:
	H = High risk
	M = Medium risk
	L = Low risk

'Timely' delivery means within the intended timeframe or a timeframe reasonably adjusted to the demands of the evolving context. In most cases, and depending on the rigour of the analysis, this may be how well the intervention was managed (operational efficiency).

Impact

What difference does the intervention make?

This is the extent to which the intervention has generated or is expected to generate significant positive or negative, intended or unintended, higher-level effects. Impact addresses the ultimate significance and potentially transformative effects of the intervention. It seeks to identify the social, environmental, and economic effects of the intervention that are longer-term or broader in scope than those already captured under the effectiveness criterion. Beyond the immediate results, this criterion seeks to capture the indirect, secondary, and potential consequences of the intervention. It does so by examining the holistic and enduring changes in systems or norms and potential effects on people's well-being, human rights, gender equality, and the environment.

Sustainability

Sustainability interrogates *whether the benefits will last.*

This is the extent to which the net benefits of the intervention continue, or are likely to continue, especially without ongoing support of a donor.

Note, that this includes an examination of the financial, economic, social, environmental, and institutional capacities of the systems needed to sustain net benefits over time and involves analyses of resilience, risks, and potential trade-offs. Depending on the timing of the evaluation, this may involve analysing the actual flow of net benefits or estimating the likelihood of net benefits continuing over the medium and long term.

How to Measure Impact and Success

When it comes to impact and success, numbers don't lie, but when it comes to actually measuring those numbers, there's some subjectivity involved, for which a bit of knowledge of data analyses and management could help. Here are a few tips on how to measure impact and success in a way that's objective and clear:

1. *Define your goals and indicators of achievements*: What exactly do you want to achieve? Without specific goals, it'll be difficult to measure impact and success. Your indicators are like milestones along your route—they tell you where you are and how far you still need to travel.
2. *Identify your metrics*: Once you know what your goals are, identify the metrics that will help you track progress towards those goals. This is about the tool of choice to measure your outcome and output indicators. Perhaps you may want to record stories of significant change from the people you've served. You may want to carry out a household survey using questionnaires (quantitative) or checklists, case studies, or before and after project video/photo evidence (qualitative).

For formal assessments and evaluations, your readers and donors will be keen to know the quality of tools used, the sample size (how many people you interviewed), their demographics, and so on. Craft your questions in a way that will elicit appropriate answers. Learn more about different types of questions and they could be presented in different formats. These could be any of these or a combination of the following: open-ended, close-ended questions, multiple choice questions, rating scale questions, Likert scale questions, matrix questions, dropdown questions, open-ended questions, demographic questions and ranking questions.

3. *Collect data*: This step is self-explanatory—gather all the data you can that relates to your chosen metrics (simply the areas you want to interrogate. This would relate to the outcome, output and potential impact of the project investments). Remember data are sensitive. Seek the acquiescence of your beneficiary and assure them of the protection of their privacy before the interview. Even more important is the need to have very highly skilled enumerators.

Often the quality of the data you get is in part directly proportionate to the way your enumerators present the questions and record and transmit them. Remember there may be a need to translate the questions into a local language for proper understanding of enumerators and especially for the respondents.

4. *Analyse the data:* Take a close look at your data and see what it's telling you about your progress towards your goals. If the tool and ways of collecting data are important, then you could say making sense of the data collected to inform meaningful interpretation is equally or even as important. The analysis tools could be as simple as using a calculator or a sheet of paper to work out addition, subtraction, fractions, and percentages to as complicated as you want it to be, depending on the target audience. Microsoft Excel and the Statistical Package for Social Scientists, also known as SPSS, are very popular data analysis tools used by project monitoring and evaluation specialists.

Having people within your team who understand these tools could make a world of difference when you present your report to your donors or share it with the global audience.

5. *Adjust your approach* and use the information collected to improve the quality of your project, as needed. Avoid overcomplication. Don't sacrifice the need for data for the need to deliver assistance to the people in need. In other words, although it's important to provide information for decision-making, my advice is to make it as simple as possible.

Based on your analysis of the data, make any necessary adjustments to ensure you're on track to achieve your goals.

Case Studies

There are a lot of different ways to measure impact and success. Here are three case studies of companies that have found success in measuring their impact.

1. *Facebook*: Since its inception, Facebook has been focused on connecting people and building relationships. The company's mission is to give people the power to share and make the world more open and connected. To measure its impact, Facebook looks at how many people are using the platform and how often they're using it. The company also looks at how many active connections people have on Facebook.
2. *Google*: Google's mission is to organise the world's information and make it universally accessible and useful. The company strives to have a positive impact on the world by making information more accessible and useful. To measure its impact, Google looks at how often people use its search engine and other products, as well as how much traffic it drives to websites around the world.
3. *Microsoft*: Microsoft's mission is to empower every person and every organisation on the planet to achieve more. The company works to help people and organisations reach their potential by creating technology that's easy to use and that works together seamlessly. To measure its impact, Microsoft looks at how its products are being used by customers and how they're helping people.

Answering these questions will require some research—asking for stories of transformation from recipients and conducting surveys and interviews with donors—but if done right, it's worth its weight in gold. We can track changes in people's lives and see how much progress we've made since our last campaign. Impact evaluation helps us measure the efficacy of our actions and develop smarter strategies for the future.

Let's take a couple of scenario examples to better explain how to measure impact:

Scenario 1: *You're a charity focused on providing education to children in low-income communities. Your initial baseline is that only five per cent of these students have access to quality education—a figure you want to raise significantly with your fundraising efforts. You'll need to set the level of change you aim to achieve. Perhaps you want to raise this to forty per cent within a period of two years.*

This means setting realistic targets for yourself and measuring whether or not you've achieved them over an agreed period of time. Being realistic cannot be overemphasised. Unrealistic targets can lead to frustration for you and your staff. There's no need to spread your resources too thin. You'll need to check back regularly and adjust your strategy accordingly; taking into account any external factors like economic hardship or changes in population size that may affect your results.

Then comes the individual element of every person your charity has affected. What stories can you share of children who have been able to access education and how can you track their progress over the same period?

Scenario 2: *You're a charity focused on providing meals to those in need. Your baseline is that, currently, forty per cent of these recipients are going hungry—a figure you want to reduce significantly through your efforts.*

You'll need to set realistic targets for yourselves and measure whether or not you've achieved them over an agreed period of time. Collecting data from people who have benefitted from your help will be key here—how has their quality of life improved since receiving meals? Are they now more likely to access jobs and other forms of support? And what strategies can you implement in the future to ensure more people benefit from your efforts?

But it's not always about hard data; sometimes, stories can be just as powerful when it comes to gauging success. We can reach out to donors or fundraisers and uncover how their efforts have made a difference in someone's life. Hearing these tales of transformation is often enough motivation to keep going, even in tough times.

Ultimately, measuring success and impact isn't an exact science; however, by setting realistic targets, gathering data from recipients, and tracking changes over time, you can obtain an accurate picture of what kind of positive change your charity is making. Knowing that you've made a difference in people's lives is all the reward you need.

Finally, don't forget to celebrate the successes—small and large. Whether that's recognising donors for their generosity or simply taking a moment to reflect on the impact your work has had on others' lives, it's an important part of any fundraising strategy. After all, if we can't give ourselves a pat on the back for our efforts, what incentive do we have to keep going?

Celebrate every win—no matter how small—and watch your charitable mission fly higher than ever!

Key Takeaways

- *Set realistic targets and track progress towards those over an agreed period of time.*
- *Ask for success stories from recipients and donors to understand the impact of your work.*
- *Measure impact by collecting data from people who have benefitted from your help.*
- *Don't forget to celebrate successes—large or small!*

Chapter 14
Sustaining Your Success

If you want to make sure your charity is around for the long haul, you need to plan for the future. That means thinking about things like succession planning, financial sustainability, and impact measurement. It may not be glamorous but it's essential if you want to keep making a difference. So don't put it off—start planning for the future today! It helps to think about how the Red Cross movement is waxing stronger and has outlived its founder.

Sustaining success is an essential part of any journey to achieving one's goals and reaching one's full potential. It requires a combination of hard work, dedication, and strategic planning to maintain and build upon successes over time.

One key aspect of sustaining success is constantly striving for improvement and growth. This means setting clear and achievable goals for yourself and regularly reviewing and revising your strategies and actions to ensure you're on track to achieving them and in tune with time. It also involves seeking out opportunities for learning and development, both formally, through education and training, and informally, through networking and seeking out mentors and role models.

Another important factor in sustaining success is having a strong support network. This can include colleagues, friends, and family members who can offer encouragement and support during challenging times and help hold you accountable to your goals and commitments. Building strong relationships with others can also help expand your horizons and expose you to new ideas and opportunities. Position your organisation by joining the right clusters, and forming strong partnerships and alliances. If you are active, truthful to your mission and can be trusted, you will be remembered.

Effective time management is also crucial for sustaining success. This involves setting clear priorities and focusing on the tasks and activities that will have the most impact on your long-term goals. It also means being mindful of the balance between personal and professional commitments and taking the time to rest and recharge when needed.

Effective communication skills are also essential for sustaining your success. This includes being able to clearly and effectively convey your ideas and thoughts to others, as well as being able to listen and understand the perspectives of others. It also involves being open to feedback and being able to adapt and adjust your approach, as needed.

Another key aspect of sustaining your success is having a strong work ethic and a positive attitude. This means being proactive, taking initiative and being willing to put in the hard work and effort required to achieve your goals. It also involves being resilient, persevering through challenges and setbacks and maintaining a positive outlook, even when things don't go as planned.

One way to sustain your success is continually seeking out new opportunities and challenges. This can involve taking on new roles or responsibilities within your current organisation or exploring new career paths and ventures. It may also involve seeking out opportunities to learn and develop new skills or collaborating with others on new projects and initiatives.

Another important factor in sustaining your success is being mindful of your physical and mental health. This means taking care of your body (and those of your team) through proper nutrition, exercise, and rest, and also taking steps to manage stress and maintain a healthy work-life balance. For your team, a policy that ensures a healthy work-life balance will help reduce burnout. It may also involve seeking out support and resources when needed, such as therapy or counselling, to help manage any mental health challenges or concerns. It is common to see people become depressed in the process of trying to play their part and do good. Charity owners and managers should not overlook this very fact.

To sustain your success, it's also important to be mindful of your personal values and priorities and to make choices and decisions that align with them. This can involve setting boundaries, being mindful of how you allocate your time and energy and being willing to make sacrifices when necessary to prioritise what's most important to you.

Finally, to sustain your success, it's essential to be adaptable and flexible. This means being open to change and being willing to pivot or adjust your approach as needed, based on new information or circumstances. It also means being open to learning and growing from your experiences and being willing to take risks and embrace new challenges.

In conclusion, sustaining your success is an ongoing process that requires a combination of hard work, dedication, and strategic planning. It involves constantly striving for improvement and growth, building a strong support network, practising effective time management, utilising excellent communication skills, maintaining a strong work ethic and positive attitude, seeking out new opportunities and challenges, taking care of your physical and mental health, being mindful of your personal values and priorities, and being adaptable and flexible. It helps to consistently work towards achieving your personal and organisational goals.

A few key areas within the organisation have to be sorted from day one. Let's look at the critical components of succession planning, financial sustainability, impact measurement, and board governance.

Succession Planning

No matter how successful your charity is today, one day it'll be time to pass the baton on to a new generation of leaders. A great way to ensure continuity and provide guidance for this transition is by creating an effective succession plan that outlines who, when, and how roles within the organisation are to be passed down. This can help reduce disruption during a leadership transition and provide assurance the legacy you built will continue with future generations.

Succession planning is the process of identifying and developing potential successors for key leadership positions within an organisation. It's a proactive approach to ensuring organisations have a competent and capable leadership team in place to continue driving business success in the future.

Effective succession planning requires a thorough understanding of an organisation's long-term goals and the skills, as well as the abilities needed to achieve those goals. It also requires a willingness to invest in the development of potential successors and foster a culture of continuous learning and growth within the organisation.

There are several key benefits to implementing a succession planning strategy. First and foremost, it helps ensure organisations have a stable and capable leadership team in place at all times. This is particularly important in times of transition, such as when a key leader retires or leaves the organisation. Without a well-defined succession plan, there's a risk the organisation will be left without the necessary leadership to drive business success.

Succession planning also helps identify and develop high-potential employees within the organisation, providing them with the necessary skills and experience to take on leadership roles in the future. This not only helps build a strong and capable leadership team but also helps retain top talent within the organisation.

In addition to the benefits to the organisation, succession planning can also be a positive experience for individual employees. It provides them with a clear career path and the opportunity to develop their skills and abilities, leading to increased job satisfaction and engagement.

However, implementing a successful succession planning strategy requires careful planning and execution. Here are some key considerations to keep in mind:

Identify key leadership positions: The first step in succession planning is identifying the key leadership positions within the organisation that are critical to its long-term success. These may include positions such as chief executive officer, chief financial officer, and other top executives, as well as department heads and key managers.

Assess current leadership capabilities: Once key positions have been identified, it's important to assess the current leadership capabilities within the organisation. This includes evaluating the skills and experience of current leaders, as well as identifying any potential gaps that need to be addressed through succession planning.

Develop a succession plan: Based on the assessment of current leadership capabilities, a succession plan can be developed to identify potential successors for each key position. This may include identifying high-potential employees within the organisation, as well as considering external candidates. The succession plan should also outline the development and training opportunities that will be provided to potential successors to ensure they're prepared for their future leadership roles.

Communicate the succession plan: Once a succession plan has been developed, it's important to communicate it to all relevant stakeholders, including current leaders, potential successors, and the rest of the organisation. This helps ensure everyone is aware of the plan and the steps being taken to ensure the future success of the organisation.

Foster a culture of continuous learning: Succession planning should not be a one-time event but rather an ongoing process. It's important to foster a culture of continuous learning and development within the organisation to ensure potential successors are continually developing the skills and experience necessary to take on leadership roles in the future.

Monitor and evaluate the succession plan: It's important to regularly review and evaluate the succession plan to ensure it meets the organisation's needs. This may include reassessing the skills and experience of potential successors and adjusting the plan, as necessary.

Succession planning can be a complex and time-consuming process but it's an essential part of any organisation's long-term success. By proactively identifying and developing potential successors for key leadership positions, organisations can ensure they have a stable and capable leadership team.

Leaders need to be groomed. Some evidence-based practices recommended for successful succession planning include creating a leadership development program, having informal mentoring sessions, and implementing job shadowing opportunities.

Leadership development programs work along the lines of building a pool of potential leaders who are groomed to take over the organisation when the time comes. This is done through providing them with training and educational experiences that enable them to gain knowledge and skills related to their current roles, as well as their future roles.

Mentoring and shadowing opportunities are also important to the succession planning process. These activities give current leaders an opportunity to spend time with and learn from potential successors while still providing them with direct feedback and guidance on their growth and development.

Financial Sustainability

Money makes the world go round and, like any other organisation, successful charities need to have financially sustainable practices in place to thrive. It's important to develop systems and processes that will ensure your charity is able to generate the income it needs to support its activities long term. Remember you started with a passion to help and make a difference, so financial stability is needed to transform your passion into realistic achievements. Many well-meaning individuals started out and later realised it takes a little more to sustain the momentum and to translate passion into sustainable actions.

It's incredibly important to develop strong fundraising skills, such as developing grant applications, launching crowdfunding campaigns, or seeking corporate partnerships, as well as building more stable revenue streams like membership fees or launching donation campaigns. For grant applications, you'll need to again hone your skill in developing impactful and fundable proposals. Major donors like the Bill and Melinda Gates Foundation, the European Union, UK Aid, USAID, some UN organs, and many corporate organisations often launch calls for proposals from time to time. Keep an eye on their websites for announcements.

Don't be shy about reaching out to professionals who have done this before for help and support. Perhaps you may not know it but many established organisations do have well-established fundraising departments that actively seek out funding opportunities to secure funding for their activities. It's often a bidding process. The organisation seeking funding is required to develop a short concept note. Then, once approved, you develop the full narrative and financial proposals for the grant.

Membership fees are by far the most reliable form of income for any charity because they provide a steady and dependable source of money that can be used to fund the work being done. Getting friends and the public to sign up and support your cause is a much more sustainable way to fund your projects.

It's also important to consider how best to manage your charity's finances. Having a clear budget and accounting system in place will enable you to track your spending and ensure donations are being spent responsibly. It's vital to be aware of where the money is coming from and going to at all times. If you're submitting an application to the major donors for project grants, these are some of the documents they'll require from you over the life cycle of your project:

- Inception report
- Baseline survey
- Quarterly report
- Interim report
- Final report
- Mid-term and final evaluation

Finally, it may be worth setting up an endowment fund so, that even if your income fluctuates, you have access to funds that can keep your project running. I have seen a vast majority of big charities having a membership roster. Members on the roster often pledge to donate an amount periodically to support the cause of your charity. By having a reserve of financial resources, you can ensure there will always be money available when it's needed most.

Infrastructure and Tools

Imagine if the Titanic had all its lifeboats, what would have happened? It's important to assess the infrastructure and tools necessary for running successful charities.

These could include elements like having a good website, email marketing software, and a customer relationship management system (CRM) for managing donors, volunteers, and partners; accounting software for tracking financial records; or volunteer management systems to manage those helping out.

It's also important to consider other technology investments that can help streamline processes such as employee time-tracking or automated donation processing. Likewise, having the physical infrastructure and a lean staff with good policies are also necessary for the successful long-term operations of any charity.

Good Governance Matters

In 2015, the National Council of Nonprofits published a report noting that "good governance and ethical leadership are essential to sustaining success." The same holds true for charities. To ensure your charity can continue to make an impact, it's important to have strong management practices in place.

We already touched on this subject earlier but it's worth revisiting the importance of having a board of directors knowledgeable about not just the mission and vision of the charity but also its legal, financial, and operational aspects.

A well-functioning board should be able to provide oversight while simultaneously being connected with the day-to-day operations. They should ensure all goals are met in an ethical manner, helping secure both the short- and long-term success of your charity.

Along with the board, staying true to the promise of delivery, ensuring all operations are compliant with the law, and having clear communication lines of authority will go a long way in creating a sustainable organisation.

Ambition Beats Perfection

There's a common saying that perfection is the enemy of good. This means striving for perfection can actually hinder progress and success because it can lead to endless tweaking and analysing, without ever actually taking action. In contrast, ambition, or the drive to succeed and achieve, can push us to take risks and make progress, even if we're not initially perfect at something. In the long run, ambition can lead to greater success and fulfilment than an obsession with perfection.

One of the main problems with perfectionism is it sets unrealistic expectations. It's human nature to want to do things well and strive for excellence, but perfectionism takes this to an extreme. It sets a standard that's often impossible to achieve, leading to feelings of inadequacy and failure, even when we've done our best. This can lead to procrastination and a lack of progress because we're too afraid to try something new or take a risk in case we don't meet the impossible standards of perfection.

Ambition also allows us to set realistic goals and work towards them with determination and perseverance. It pushes us to take action and make progress, even if we're not initially perfect at something. This can lead to a sense of accomplishment and satisfaction, as we see the results of our hard work and dedication.

Another issue with perfectionism is it often leads to a lack of flexibility and adaptability. When we're so focused on achieving perfection, we may become inflexible and unwilling to adapt or change our approach. This can be detrimental in a rapidly changing world because we need to be able to adapt and pivot to stay relevant and successful.

Ambition, in contrast, allows us to be open to new ideas and approaches. It pushes us to constantly improve and seek out new opportunities, rather than becoming stuck in a narrow-minded pursuit of perfection. This flexibility and adaptability can lead to greater success and growth in the long run.

Additionally, perfectionism can lead to a lack of creativity and innovation. When we're so focused on achieving perfection, we may become too afraid to try new things or take creative risks. This can stifle our creativity and prevent us from coming up with new and innovative ideas.

Ambition, in contrast, allows us to be bold and take risks. It pushes us to think outside the box and come up with new and creative solutions to problems. This willingness to try new things and take risks can lead to greater innovation and success in the long run.

Furthermore, perfectionism can lead to a lack of collaboration and teamwork. When we're so focused on achieving perfection, we may become too concerned with our own work and not be open to feedback or ideas from others. This can lead to a lack of collaboration and teamwork because we're not willing to consider the perspectives of others.

Ambition also allows us to be open to feedback and ideas from others. It pushes us to work as a team and collaborate to achieve our goals. This teamwork and collaboration can lead to greater success and growth because we're able to combine our strengths and expertise to achieve common goals.

In conclusion, although perfectionism may seem like a desirable trait, it can actually hinder progress and success. In contrast, ambition, or the drive to succeed and achieve, can push us to take risks and make progress, even if we're not initially perfect at something. In the long run, ambition can lead to greater success and fulfilment than an obsession with perfection.

Sustaining your success as a charity is no easy feat—it often feels like you're running a marathon, not just a sprint. Although there are countless elements to consider when putting together the plans for the future of your organisation, one thing is certain: ambition beats perfection.

An ambition to make a lasting impact and make a difference in the world is what will help you stay focused and motivated. It's easy to get caught up in the details but remember your primary aim should always be making the most positive impact possible.

It's essential to understand that, sometimes, it may take time to reach your goals, but with consistent effort and dedication, anything can be achieved. With ambition driving you forward, there's no limit to what you can achieve for your charity.

At the end of the day, the goal is to last.

Key Takeaways

- *The key to sustaining success for a charity lies in having a clear plan for the future, establishing good governance practices, and having an ambition to make lasting change.*
- *It's important to ensure there are adequate resources available at all times, including infrastructure and tools, as well as financial reserves.*
- *Having a board of directors with knowledge of the legal, financial, and operational aspects of the charity can help guide your organisation towards long-term sustainability.*
- *Ambition beats perfection—it's essential to stay focused on making the most positive impact possible while being realistic about how much time it may take to reach certain goals.*

Bibliography

Badewi, A., Management of Risk Module, University of Kent.

Balanced Score Card, Strategic Planning Basics, Accessed 16 April 2023. https://balancedscorecard.org/strategic-planning-basics/

Barua, S., Kar, D., Mahbub, F. (2018) 'Risks and Their Management in Ready-Made Garment Industry: Evidence from the World's Second Largest Exporting Nation', 24, 75-103, 10.6347/JBM.201809_24(2).0004.

Bennett, R. (2005) 'Implementation Processes and Performance Levels of Charity Internet Fundraising Systems', Journal of Marketing Channels, 12(3), 53-77.

Calhoun, J. (2020) 'I'm Productivity Expert Charles Duhigg, and This is How I Work', Lifehacker, Accessed 6 Jan. 2023. https://lifehacker.com/im-productivity-expert-charles-duhigg-andthis-is-how-1844561632

Charity Navigator, 'Donor Resources Charity Navigator', Accessed 6 Jan. 2023. https://www.charitynavigator.org/donorbasics/

Chevalier, J. M., Buckles, D. J. (2012) Participatory Action Research, Theory and methods for engaged inquiry, Problem Tree, Wageningen University Publication. https://mspguide.org/2022/03/18/problem-tree/

Concern Worldwide, 'Who We Are', Accessed 18 Feb. 2023. https://www.concern.net/who-we-are/our-history

Concern Worldwide (2019) 'Our History', Accessed 6 Jan. 2023. https://www.concern.net/who-we-are/our-history

Poate, D., Barnett, C. (2003) 'Measuring Value for Money? An independent review of DFID's Value for Money (VFM) Indicator, Public Service Agreement 2003-2006', DFID Evaluation Report EV 645, Accessed 26 Jan. 2023.

Doctors Without Borders, USA (2016) 'Report: Ebola 20142015 Facts and Figures', Accessed 6 Jan. 2023.

https://www.doctorswithoutborders.org/latest/report-ebola2014-2015-facts-and-figures.

Encyclopaedia Britannica (2019) 'Helen Keller International', Accessed 18 Dec. 2023. https://www.britannica.com/topic/Helen-Keller-International

European Union (2018) PM² Project Management Methodology Guide 3.0, doi: 10.2799/755246.

Hillman, B. J. (2014) 'Mission, Vision, and Values', *Journal of the American College of Radiology*, 11(1), 3.

Kotter, J. P. (1996) *Leading Change*, Boston: Harvard Business School Press.

Laoyan, S. (2022) 'Understanding the Pareto Principle (The 80/20 Rule)', Asana, Accessed 6 Jan. 2023. https://asana.com/resources/pareto-principle-80-20-rule.

Marie Stopes International Reproductive Choices, 'Our History', Accessed 6 Jan. 2023. https://www.msichoices.org/whowe-are/our-history/

More, R. (2021) 'Choosing a Type of Nonprofit Organisation', Legalzoom. Accessed 6 Jan. 2023. https://www.legalzoom.com/articles/choosing-a-type-ofnonprofit-organisation

Mother Teresa Foundation, 'About Us', Accessed 18 Nov. 2022. https://motherteresafoundation.org/about/

OECD, 'DAC Criteria Evaluation of Development Programme', Development Co-operation Directorate, Accessed 4 Dec. 2022. https://www.oecd.org/dac/evaluation/daccriteriaforevaluatingdevelopmentassistance.htm.

OXFAM, 'Our History', Accessed 6 Jan. 2023. https://www.oxfam.org/en/our-history

Real, C. C. (2010) 'Oxfam International', *In International Encyclopaedia of Civil Society*, edited by Anheier, H. K., Toepler, S., p. 1122-1123. New York, NY: Springer US.

Red Cross, 'Who We Are', Accessed 6 Jan. 2023. https://www.icrc.org/en/whowe-are/history/founding.

Red Cross (2008) 'Red Cross Our History', Accessed 6 Jan. 2023. https://www.redcross.org/about-us/who-weare/history.html

Resource Centre UK (2009) 'Legal Structures for Community Groups and Not-for-Profit Organisations', Accessed 6 Jan. 2023. https://www.resourcecentre.org.uk/information/legal-structuresfor-community-and-voluntary-groups/

Survey Monkey, 'Types of survey questions', Accessed 1 Nov. 2022. https://www.surveymonkey.com/mp/survey-question-types/

University of Wolverhampton, An Introduction to Multi-Agency Planning Using the Logical Framework Approach Developed by: 0-19+ Partnership and the Centre for International Development and Training (CIDT).

Theory of Change (2011) 'What is Theory of Change?' Accessed 6 Oct. 2022. https://www.theoryofchange.org/what-is-theory-ofchange/

The World Association of Non-Governmental Organisations (WANGO), Worldwide NGO Directory, 'About', Accessed 30 Dec. 2022. https://www.wango.org/about.aspx.

Value Prop, 'the-actionable-swot-analysis'. https://www.valueprop.com/blog/the-actionable-swot-analysis.